As the Sorcerer Said . . .

Also in this series

1 *Violence* Festus Iyayi
2 *Firebrands* Sahle Sellassie
3 *In the Castle of My Skin* George Lamming
4 *Ways of Sunlight* Samuel Selvon
5 *A Brighter Sun* Samuel Selvon
6 *The Lonely Londoners* Samuel Selvon
7 *Bukom* Bill Marshall
8 *Muriel at Metropolitan* Miriam Tlali
9 *Cascades* Jared Angira
10 *A Smell of Onions* Peggy Appiah
11 *Edufa* Efua T. Sutherland
12 *Jingala* Legson Kayira
13 *Farewell to Babylon* Bode Sowande
14 *The Victims* Isidore Okpewho
15 *Sundiata: An Epic of Old Mali* D. T. Niane
16 *No Sweetness Here* Ama Ata Aidoo
17 *The Marriage of Anansewa* Efua T. Sutherland
18 *The Bushtrackers* Meja Mwangi
19 *Anowa* Ama Ata Aidoo
20 *Flowers and Shadows* Ben Okri
21 *Bozambo's Revenge* Bertène Juminer
22 *A Decade of Tongues* J. P. Clark
23 *Snares Without End* Olympe Bhêly-Quénum
24 *The Poet Lied* Odia Ofeimun
25 *Cross of Gold* Lauretta G. Ngcobo
26 *The Dragon Can't Dance* Earl Lovelace
27 *The Dilemma of a Ghost* Ama Ata Aidoo
28 *Tropical Circle* Alioum Fantouré
29 *The Feud* R. Sarif Easmon
30 *Old Story Time* Trevor Rhone
31 *The Beggars' Strike* Aminata Sow Fall
33 *Jazz and Palm Wine* edited by Willfried F. Feuser
34 *The Contract* Festus Iyayi
35 *Our Sister Killjoy* Ama Ata Aidoo
36 *Danny Boy* James Bradner
37 *The Last Duty* Isidore Okpewho
38 *The Landscapes Within* Ben Okri
39 *Fireflies* Shiva Naipaul
40 *Third World Poems* Edward Kamau Brathwaite
41 *My Cousin Comes to Jo'burg* Mbulelo Mzamane
42 *Call Me Not A Man* Mtutuzeli Matshoba
43 *A Son of the Soil* Wilson Katiyo
44 *The Crocodile* Vincent Eri
45 *Going to Heaven* Wilson Katiyo
47 *The Whirlwind* F. Byomuhangi
48 *A Dakar Childhood* Nafissatou Diallo
55 *My Bones and My Flute* Edgar Mittelholzer
56 *The Chip-Chip Gatherers* Shiva Naipaul
58 *Behind the Clouds* Ifeoma Okoye
59 *The Mocking Stones* Prince Dowu Palmer
60 *The Children of Soweto* Mbulelo Vizikhungo Mzamane
63 *Thought-Tracks* Musaemura Bonas Zimunya

As the Sorcerer Said . . .

Myriam Warner-Vieyra

translated by
Dorothy S. Blair

Longman

Longman Group Limited,
Longman House,
Burnt Mill, Harlow, Essex, UK

First published in Paris in 1980 by Présence Africaine as *Le Quimboiseur L'Avait Dit...*
First published in Longman Drumbeat 1982

ISBN 0 582 78557 X

Print in Hong Kong by
Sing Cheong Printing Co. Ltd.

'Where confidence leads you,
strength will not save you'

(Caribbean proverb)

This is a story which might have begun: 'Once upon a time, there was a little girl who lived in a tiny little village on an island that was as big as two coconuts.

'Her mother was the most beautiful person in the village, and her father was a fisherman who sometimes took the little girl out to sea with him. . . .

'She had a friend who was the smartest little boy on the island, the one who always knew everything. They ran barefoot and bareheaded all over the island.

'They swam in the river, gorged themselves on fruit, saturated themselves with sunshine. . . .'

And then the story would end: 'The little girl grew up to be as beautiful as her mother, married the clever little boy and they lived happily ever after and had lots of children.'

In fact it didn't turn out like this at all.

Some people will say it was fate. . . . Do you believe in fate?

It was a large, rectangular room with five beds on each side of a central gangway that went down the whole length. A table and two wooden benches were set out in the middle. Four windows broke the uniformity of the walls. The whiteness of the walls, ceiling, beds, sheets, the table and two benches hurt my eyes after a night spent in total darkness.

I couldn't make out what I was doing in this room; I didn't know these white girls, in unbleached holland nightdresses, who occupied the other beds. So where was I? Certainly very far from home, from all those who are dear to me. . . . On my left, a girl of about my own age, fifteen or sixteen, smiled at me. She had a very sweet expression; her nose was a bit long for such a young face which was framed in long golden curls. Her curls reminded me of something. . . . My island! The curled wood shavings that I loved to watch flying from under Mr Sostene's plane! Good old Mr Sostene was the village carpenter. He was as happy repairing things as making new ones: huts, fishing-boats, furniture, anything made of wood that anyone gave him orders for. 'You can't tell me anything about wood,' he used to say, by way of finalising an order.

'Are you feeling better?' the girl asked me.

'Yes. . . .'

Dozens of hammers were hammering hundreds of nails into my head which felt as heavy as a newly gathered calabash. I couldn't really understand what she meant. . . . 'Where are we?'

'Oh, yes, of course! You got here very late last night, and you were completely out! This is Dr Cousin's ward in the Charity Hospital.'

'Hospital! I'm not ill, not as far as I know. . . .'

The girl in the bed at the end of the row, nearest the door, shouted, 'Look out!' and all the girls who were out of bed, chattering, were back under their blankets in the twinkling of an eye.

A group of about ten people, men and women in white coats, entered. They were all hanging on the words of a tall, dried-up looking man with a shiny bald head. He stopped for varying lengths of time beside each bed. This was Professor Cousin himself. The person who must have been the sister-in-charge noted everything this man said on a large sheet of paper, fixed to a thin board. He spoke very softly and I could only catch a few words of what he said about the girls on each side of me; in the one case, the dose of a drug with an impossible name had to be diminished and electroconvulsive therapy begun. As for the blonde girl on my left, he said she had to continue with the same doses of trimethadione.

When he came to me, Professor Cousin said, 'How is our little island flower?' and tapped me on the cheek, which seemed to increase the number of nails hammered into my head. Then he turned to a young coloured man I hadn't noticed before and said, 'You look after her, Edward, she'll be more at ease with you.'

'Yes, sir.'

Then, turning towards the nurse who was taking notes, Edward said, 'Sister Melin, bring her to me at the end of the round.'

When the group had gone, the girl on my left came and sat on the edge of my bed and went on explaining things to me. She didn't go on talking very long, as I had closed my eyes because the light in the room hurt them. She thought I had fallen asleep and went away.

In fact, I did not care whether I was here or anywhere else in this country, since I was alone and far from my island. My truth was a lie, and their brisk lies seemed to smell more of truth. Everything started to come back to me: the scene which had broken out two days ago, the night spent in the police station, my arrival, heavily sedated, in this room which seemed like something out of a strange dream, peopled with fantastic faces and forms.

'Days of disaster send no warning before them.'

No, I would not think of the present. This whole

business was more than I could understand. I had to put off as long as possible 'the moment of truth', in order to keep the present at bay.

I directed my thoughts towards my village which I ought never to have left. This tiny fishing village from which the sea, while being the source of life, occasionally claimed an experienced fisherman. My grandfather and my father's only brother had disappeared like this one night when the seas ran high. I was very young, but at the sight of my parents' worried faces and those of the other village folk, I understood that the sea had claimed their precious lives and that they would never come back again.

As soon as it was light, the *lambi* conch-shells rang out their mournful message from hill to hill, announcing the sad news to the neighbouring hamlets. For several days our house was invaded with crowds of people. All evening the men played dice under the flickering oil lamps on the veranda, or else spent their time in terrifying games of skill, like the one that consists of plunging a penknife faster and faster in between outstretched fingers. Sometimes one man would recount the adventures of Brer Rabbit, or tell stories about the she-devils that lived in the mountains. The women, in between telling their rosaries dozens of times, served rum and coffee, wept, heaved deep sighs or else laughed at the comic stories the man was telling, then begged pardon of the dead for having laughed. Finally there was silence, a heavy, solemn silence that my little voice could not break. And life resumed its course, under the smiling sunshine of my village.

My head no longer ached and I let myself sink into a gentle doze, the passport to dreams in which I was back home in Cocotier.

Cocotier was a straggling little village on the island of Karura, about ten miles to the north of Bonne Terre, that we simply referred to as 'the Town'. We went to Town or we came back from Town, and its name was of little importance as it was the only town that we knew. All the inhabitants of our village had been to town at least once in their lives. Cocotier had no more than twenty houses in all, of which about half lined the principal street, which was the only one suitable for vehicles.

Most of the inhabitants of the village, including ourselves, gained their livelihood from the sea. Our house, like all the others, was a hut made entirely out of wood. It has four rooms now, but originally there were only two, with a veranda in front. As children were born and the family grew larger, my father had two little rooms built on at the back: one for the girls and the other for the boys.

The main room was sparsely furnished with a rectangular table made of brown wood, grown shiny with age and from polishing with the coconut straw that we used to clean the furniture, the partitions and floors. Six wooden chairs stood round this table. One still had its cane seat and stood on its four legs; the others, with the passage of time, had had their cane seats replaced by wooden planks and stood on three legs. Some wooden shelves served as a dresser and proudly displayed two glass tumblers standing between our enamel beakers and plates. In one corner, on an empty soap-box, various objects, including a jar of drinking water, were placed. Above the front door hung a picture of the archangel Michael laying low a black, horned devil and gazing down at us from his chipped gold frame.

The walls were decorated with pictures cut out of old magazines. My favourite one showed a pretty white lady in a grey coat and hat, a strange street with bright lights and a tower constructed entirely of criss-crossing iron girders. Underneath was written 'Evening in Paris, Cheramy'.

An imposing iron-barred bed occupied the place of honour in the dead centre of my father's room. The paint that had once covered it had long given way to rust. At the foot of the bed stood a wardrobe that had lost the mirror from its door. An old trunk in one corner held the family treasures: books, photographs, 'important' papers, yellow with age.

The only furniture in the rooms for us children was a set of wooden shelves and some nails to hang our clothes on. There were no doors and no beds. When night fell, each child spread out a pile of rags in a corner and lay down.

Cooking was done in the open, behind the house; a sheet of iron protected the hearth that consisted of three large stones of even size, on which we placed our clay pots to cook our food. . . .

Our hut was the last on the road going north. Our nearest neighbour on the left was Mr Felix who ran the local bus linking our village and the nearby hamlets with the town. Mrs Felix kept the only bar and general store in the area, 'Chez Lorvilia'. Lorvilia was her Christian name but we all called her Mrs Felix.

The shop consisted of a rectangular room. A zinc counter occupied the whole width in front of a double door that opened on to the road. At the back, the part reserved for the bar was furnished with three tables of polished wood and a few stools, masterpieces of Mr Sostene's art. A curtain of thin bamboo strips danced merrily in the wind, separating the shop from the bar.

Seffini, a young woman from the neighbouring village of Bananier, helped Mrs Felix in the shop and served in the bar in the evenings. Seffini was a lusty, strapping great wench with a ready tongue in her head. She owed her curious name to the fact that she was the last of a family of fourteen children, her mother having decided that that was enough: '*C'est fini!*'

She had certainly not inherited her mother's great fertility since, at the age of thirty, in spite of many services rendered to the local bachelors, her belly had never rivalled her rump in prominence.

To the right of our house, an enormous coconut plantation surrounded our village on three sides. This must have been the reason for its name. A few yards from the house the clear ribbon of the river Corossol flowed into the sea.

Behind Cocotier there were fields and higher up, perched on the side of a bluff, was the hamlet of Corossol, near which my grandmother's hut and allotment were situated. Finally, still higher, one came to the forest and the mysterious mountain.

I had never been to the top of this mountain. Right at the top there were said to be huge pools of boiling water and burning craters. People also said that a long time ago a young man from our village was coming back from a dance in Corossol when he met a beautiful girl who asked him to go back home with her. After they had walked for more than an hour and he could no longer recognise the area, he became suspicious and refused to go any further, deciding to stay where he was till daybreak. The girl grew angry, slapped her companion's face and went away. When the sun rose, the young man saw that he had stopped a few feet from one of these pools of boiling water and he realised that the beautiful girl was one of the mountain she-devils.

Opposite our house, as soon as you crossed the road, there was the infinite ocean, so blue and transparent that we could see the little fish dancing about our feet without even putting our heads under the water. The sand here was a pearly grey, the only side of the island where the sand was this colour. A little further to the north, at Raisin Clair, it was fine and white. We used to go there sometimes on Sundays, after Mass. That was our big outing. The Raisin Clair beach was covered for miles with sea-grapes, coco-plums and sea-almonds and we would pick a huge supply to last us the whole week. We used to buy 'snowballs' made of chips of grated ice with syrup poured over, and coconut sorbets. This was the townsfolk's favourite beach.

The town! I didn't know it very well. Once, at Mardi Gras, we had gone in Mr Felix's bus to watch the procession of floats decorated with flowers. In the town there were houses built of brick with more than one storey. There was a big square called Coco-plum Field, which was carpeted with closely cut lawns and lined with almond trees and royal palms that were at least 150 feet high. In the middle there was a stone statue of a very tall white woman with a small soldier beside her; underneath was written: 'The Mother Country to her Children who died for France, 1914–1918; 1939–1945'.

Various bands played for the dancers who were perched on the floats. They wore fancy costumes; some were dressed up as flowers or as Chinamen and one was a French king in a periwig, but the best were the beautiful Creole girls wearing traditional costume. There were a lot of white people in town. My mother had gone off with one of these white men. People said that he had taken her to France because she would be a great success there, as she was very beautiful and not very dark-skinned. . . .

We often talked about colour at home. My father was one of the darkest people in the village and my mother among the lightest.

We were four children. My youngest brother Jose took after my father and was the darkest in the family; my mother didn't love him and never kissed him like she kissed Louis who was the lightest. My sister Zelia and I had the sort of complexion that people called 'sapodilla plum' which didn't offend the whites and the half-castes who didn't like people to be too black. So I'd never heard any comments on my colour, or felt any hostility from Mother – nothing that I can remember today.

Mother went off some time after 14 July 1946. People said it was at the dance at the village hall to celebrate Bastille Day that the white man had picked her out. They danced together many times. She was very fond of white folk, just the opposite of my father. It's true that her own father had been white. He was the son of the people my grandmother had worked for as a general servant from the age of twelve. She was scarcely seventeen when the spoilt son of these people had put her in the family way. The parents dismissed her as soon as her belly became too conspicuous, though they continued to pay her wages every month for a long time, to satisfy their conscience. So she didn't need to work for white folk any more. Since then she had lived off a little plot of ground that she bought with some of the money her former employers had sent her. Once a week she came down to town to sell her fruit and vegetables in the market.

My father didn't like the whites but he didn't hate them either. He thought we shouldn't mix with these 'red-ears'. 'What's good for the goat isn't good for the sheep', he would say, and 'The cockroach is never in the right if the hen is around', so a Negro is never in the right as far as a white man is concerned. 'If a white man farts, they throw the nigger out', he would also say.

As far as I was concerned, I couldn't understand why we weren't all made the same colour, which would have simplified things. How did it happen that we were black rather than white? Our first history lesson that year happened to be about 'our ancestors the Gauls, with their blue eyes and fair hair'. Why were we black? I put the question to our teacher, Miss Ida, and she replied, 'God wanted it that way'. When I asked her why God hadn't made us like our ancestors the Gauls, she walked away without answering. Since then I never dared talk about this, for there are some questions that it is not a good thing to ask. . . .

My mother left at six o'clock one morning in Mr Felix's bus, which always left at that time for town. In the evening Mr Felix brought back a letter from Mother for my father, saying she was going off to Paris with Mr Milan, the white man who had been at the July 14th dance, and that she had known him for a long time as they had been at high school together.

Father never said anything to us about this letter. When it came to explaining Mother's departure he said she had gone to work in an office in town as she had had an education. But we knew the true facts of the matter from Mr Felix's son who was always well up with all the gossip that his father brought back from town.

In fact, I knew before Father the exact date when Mother sailed from our country on the *Catoumba*, the boat that linked our island with the port of Le Havre in France, taking ten days to do the crossing.

I was probably the only one to feel genuinely sad,

possibly because I was the eldest; I understood better what had happened, and I was fond of Mother. She was so pretty you had to forgive her for being bad-tempered sometimes, especially with Father. She often told him he was a narrow-minded, uneducated nigger. Father never said anything, which upset me most of all. He would always smile and never get worked up or react to insults. With his friends he always spoke in the same controlled way. I often used to see him nod his head and smile at the jokes some of them would make. If he were asked his opinion he would reply in the least possible number of words, as if he wanted to ration them. More often than not the only sounds he made were 'nn-nn!' for no and 'nn-hnn!' for yes. He always looked serious and sad. And yet he was a very handsome man with regular features and a small mouth which wasn't anything like those you usually find in very dark-skinned Negroes. He was of average height and carried himself like a young sporting type, in spite of his hard work.

Someone called my name and touched my hand, or rather took my pulse. It was the nurse who had been taking notes a few moments ago. She smiled at me. 'Come along now! We're going to see Dr Edward, he wants to have a chat with you, he's very nice.'

I tried to get out of bed but the whole room started spinning round and I had to shut my eyes. I bravely put one foot on the ground and opened one eye, then the other, and things began to settle down. Sister Melin helped me walk the few yards from my bed to the middle of the room where she put me in a wheelchair and wrapped a rug round me.

We went through the door on the right, through another equally large ward filled with girls who seemed much younger, between eight and twelve years old, and through two other doors, the last of which was locked. Sister Melin opened it with a big flat key and locked it behind us.

We crossed a large square courtyard surrounded with buildings. Male and female nurses were coming and going, accompanying patients, some walking, some in wheelchairs. Many of these patients were men and women who looked worn out, as if they had got to the end of their lives. Their pallid complexions and vacant expressions made you think of ghosts, rather than human beings.

Others, I don't know why, were fat with puffy faces, like pigs at carnival time in Cocotier. It was rather chilly. I could see the sky which wasn't a bit like the sky on my island. It was quite grey; there was no sun; where had it hidden itself . . .? The walls were the same colour as the sky. The blankets wrapped round the patients in wheelchairs were as grey as the bark of the few skeletons of trees that were visible, all leafless and with branches twisted in agony from the suffering inflicted on them by the climate of this country.

We reached the building on the opposite side of the courtyard from ours. There, there were some flowers and a few shrubs which still retained their leaves. People in outdoor clothes were waiting in a big entrance hall, looking very resigned. Those patients who, like me, arrived with a nurse, went down a large corridor with doors on both sides, each with a number on it.

We stopped in front of one of these doors; on it was a big notice saying 'Medical Officer' and a bit lower down was pinned a visiting card with the name 'Dr Edward Bali'. Sister Melin knocked and we went in immediately.

Dr Edward was sitting at a table that was clearly too small for all it had to hold. Piles of books and files were balanced precariously and there was only a tiny free space, about eighteen inches square. The doctor was writing something that I couldn't make out in a hieroglyphic handwriting on a blank sheet of paper.

Sister Melin helped me out of the wheelchair into a fairly high leather armchair; she pressed a pedal and the chair slid back halfway into a very comfortable, restful position.

'Come back in half an hour,' the doctor said to her when he had finished what he was writing. Then he came over to me and sat down on a metal stool placed next to my chair.

'So, how do you feel today?'

'All right. . . .'

At least that was the only correct thing I could come out with.

He took my pulse and looked into the whites of my eyes.

'No anaemia. Once you've got over the fatigue and all the excitement, you'll be all right. Fine. Now we're going to chat like two old friends. How old are you?'

'Nearly sixteen.'

'You've been in France a month, haven't you?'

'Yes. . . .'

I couldn't understand why he was asking me all these questions to which he already knew the answers.

He lit a cigarette, stood up, took a few steps towards his desk, turned and came back to me, stopped and smiled.

'Your parents say that you couldn't get used to life in France and that you were behaving very aggressively.'

'My parents! What parents? I haven't got any family here. I'm all alone. The people I was living with never treated me like their child. . . . If you only knew!'

I burst into sobs. It was not from unhappiness; I was weeping from rage and frustration.

'Yes, but the lady said she was your mother.'

'It's probably the only time she's admitted that I'm her daughter. . . . I was their servant. Don't talk to me about them!'

'Calm yourself. You know I want to help you to see clearly into your own mind; to do this you must tell me yourself, in your own words, everything that has happened since you arrived in France. . . . We'll leave it at that for today. When you leave hospital, what would you like to do?'

'Catch the first boat back home,' I said firmly.

Dr Edward didn't look surprised, as if he had expected my reply even before he asked the question. After a heavy silence that lasted a few moments, he went over to his desk and carefully stubbed out his cigarette in an ashtray that was already overflowing. Then he came and sat down again on the stool next to me.

'You see, you mustn't discard all the other possibilities. Unfortunately, you've only experienced the bad side of France. Paris is a depressing city for a girl who has been used to living close to nature, like you. If you had the chance to know a different aspect of life here, you'd change your mind. For example, you could go to boarding school, continue your studies and train for a career. You could live with girls of your own age, far from Paris, in the country where there are trees and fields. I think you would like that very much. What do you think . . .?'

'Perhaps . . . I don't know . . . I'm so tired . . . Just now, all I want is to sleep. . . .'

'Very well! You shall sleep if you want to. I'll see you tomorrow at the same time. There's no hurry after all. . . .'

I wasn't really sleepy, I didn't want to talk about the present or the future, I wasn't ready to look reality in the face. I was afraid of all this solitude, all the degradation in which I had become enveloped over the past month. I needed to steep myself in my past life, in Cocotier, just as we used to soak ourselves in a bath of certain green leaves back home, to wash away the effects of the evil eye and regain our high spirits with the return of good luck. I would have liked this month in France never to have existed. To wake up clean after a dream in which I had been floundering in a ditch full of shit and say to myself, with a sigh of relief, 'It was only a dream!' I feel sick if I think of all that filth now, I'm sure I'm going to vomit like that day when we were playing hide-and-seek and I found myself face to face with the putrefying carcass of a dead cat. My stomach heaved up all its contents, spontaneously, without my having any control over myself. It was during the long holidays, the year my mother went away.

Dr Edward had gone back to his table. I closed my eyes, to pick up my dream again where it had been interrupted a little while before by Sister Melin; I was back on my island.

A few days after Mother's departure, my grandmother came to live with us, as Father, like most of the men in our village, was a fisherman. He left home at dawn and only came back late in the afternoon and I was far too young at ten to be a real mother to my younger brothers.

Grandma was a tiny little woman, quite thin and very energetic. She cultivated her allotment all by herself and made a living from the different vegetables that she grew for sale. She was very kind to us and took pride in her appearance and in no time she had transformed our home.

Every evening the women of the village came over to us to chat. There was singing and laughter. Even my father acquired a slightly richer vocabulary than I had ever known him to possess.

Mr Felix's son, who knew everything that was said in the village, told me that the local people preferred my grandmother, who was one of them, to my mother, who had always put on grand airs as she had been to the big school in town, the one where you could get your School Certificate. There were also rumours that she had never forgiven my grandmother for having married her off to a fisherman who could scarcely read and, what was worse, one of the darkest-skinned men in the village.

Gradually my brothers and my sister Zelia forgot Mother, and later on I did too. As for Father, he could be heard whistling as he mended his nets and I could have quite a normal conversation with him. Now he used to go out every evening after supper and meet his friends in Mrs Felix's bar, 'Chez Lorvilia'. The men used to congregate there to drink rum, smoke and play dominoes. Some of them stumbled home quite late at night, drunk with alcohol but also from the exhaustion of a heavy day at sea.

I had never seen my father drunk; perhaps he was as sensible as Mr Felix who only drank two glasses, never three, as he had to drive and was 'in charge of people's souls'. And if Father had got drunk and made scenes like Papa Mano, then Mr Felix's son would certainly have told me, as he missed nothing. From the height of his twelve years, he was full of mischief and sparkling with intelligence, and he was already in the class with the big boys and girls at our local school, whereas the other children of his age were still in the lower section.

Our school was a big hut, bigger than any of the other buildings in the village. It was next to the church and the village hall, surrounded by a beautiful hedge of cayenne roses and a lovely flowerbed.

In front there were two big classrooms. The two teachers lived at the back: Miss Ida, who was our teacher in the lower division, and Mrs Paule who taught the three rows of children in the upper division.

Each of these two big rooms was divided into three rows. Each row represented a class. I was in the third row of the lower division, the beginners, which must have corresponded to standard three of the primary school. My youngest brother Jose was in the second row of my section and Mr Felix's son was in the second row of the upper division, with the big pupils, which was the equivalent of standard five. The third row of the big boys' and girls' division corresponded to standard six. If you passed your primary exam at the end of that year you could go to the big school in town and take your School Certificate.

However, very few children in our village had any ambition to continue their education. Sometimes the boys even left school before they had passed their primary certificate, and went fishing with their fathers or helped in the fields. Or else they were expelled by Mrs Paule, who took any excuse to get rid of a pupil: if they hadn't learned their lessons, if they arrived late, or once, because someone had an attack of giggles when Mrs Paule caught her dress on a nail.

I didn't suffer too much after all from Mother's departure and two years later my memory of this event was already rather blurred. Nobody ever mentioned her. I was really curious to know if she had become a success in Paris, as she was very beautiful.

Father looked much happier. Grandma and the other women kept saying that they ought to find another wife for him; but he said he didn't want a wife as he was all right with his children and his boat, *By God's Grace*. But I suspected him of having a few affairs in the neighbouring hamlet of Corossol where he sometimes went in the evening, after supper, with the excuse that he needed a bit of a walk. One evening I saw him select a fine bream before setting off on his walk. And he'd taken the trouble to have a bath and put on clean clothes.

There was a knock at the door. Sister Melin entered. She had come to fetch me back.

The doctor got up and walked round his office. 'Bring her back tomorrow morning at ten o'clock. No sleeping pills.'

And turning towards me, he held out both his hands with a broad smile and said, 'Goodbye for now, Suzette. I'll see you tomorrow.'

I tried to smile back. My heart wasn't in it and I must have made a horrible grimace. I heard a hoarse voice murmur, 'Goodbye, doctor', and realised with astonishment that it was my own voice I had just heard.

We went back without speaking a word. In the big courtyard a pale sun made the grey colour of the buildings look even more pallid. There was the same bustle of activity as before. This time men and women were pushing big trolleys laden with enormous, steaming cooking pots, bread and jugs filled with water. All these people were coming out of the last building before ours, where the kitchens must have been.

I could now see our building completely and realised that it was quite different from all the others. It had only one storey and seemed to have been built quite recently as the walls were of a darker grey than the rest.

Except for one main door, the only openings were the barred windows which had very thick panes, letting in a little light, but not allowing anyone to see out. Sister Melin opened the door with her big key.

A pungent smell that I couldn't quite place – a mixture of medicines, cleaning materials and cabbage soup – greeted me as we entered.

Some of the girls were sitting on their beds, chatting; others were reading or sleeping. Two of the beds were empty and had not been made. I learnt later that the occupants had left the hospital to return to their families.

I felt very weak. For the past few moments I had become aware of the cause of this weakness: I was starving and very thirsty; I had eaten nothing for more than twenty-four hours. The sight of the steaming stewpots and the bread on the trolleys in the courtyard had excited my stomach which had begun to rumble particularly noisily.

The girl in the bed on my left greeted me with a big smile.

'Now then! What's your name?'

'Suzette.'

'Oh! What a pretty name! It's quite exotic.'

Since I'd been in this country I'd heard this word more than ten times; everything to do with me seemed to be 'exotic'. Once I'd asked what the word meant. That made my mother blush with shame; she didn't like me to ask questions that showed me up for an ignorant nigger-girl.

'My name's Sarah. I'm not really ill, you know . . . I have blackouts; it can be serious, depending on the circumstances. Once I was riding my bicycle and I fell off. Fortunately it was in the country on a road where there was hardly any traffic. . . .'

Her words bubbled out like a mountain spring; I took advantage of a very brief pause to get a word in.

'What's a blackout?'

'You'll see; I don't have so many now, scarcely two or three a day. . . . Anyway, if I do have one, don't worry, it isn't serious and I always come round in a few seconds.'

Was it the fact of having talked about her blackouts that set one off? Suddenly she stopped short in the middle of a word, her eyes flickering, her mouth half-open. The book she was holding slipped out of her hands which jerked convulsively. If she hadn't warned me I would certainly have thought she was dying. After a few seconds she came round, looking completely disorientated for a moment, then picked up her book.

I was going to take advantage of this to doze off again when the door on the right opened and one of the trolleys I had seen in the courtyard appeared, pushed by a huge black woman. She was a great hulk of a woman, like a veritable barrel of rum. She was wearing a grey overall and a headscarf which half hid her straightened hair. She had lipstick on her thick lips. She was like an enormous doll. Several of the girls greeted her with 'Hello, Doudou!' She replied, 'Hello, my little treasures.' A small dark-haired girl from the row of beds opposite me got down to help Doudou; she passed the trays to those who couldn't or wouldn't get out of bed. The others took their trays and went to sit at the big rectangular table.

When she had finished Doudou came over to my bed.

'Hello, daughter! Where do you come from?'

'Karura.'

'Well now! So do I. You still got the same accent like the folks back home. It's a pleasure to hear you. How long you been in France?'

'About a month.'

'Well, that's nice. I been here for twenty years. My name's Leontine, but the people here likes to give you a nickname. They all call me Doudou, from the superintendent right down to the cleaners. Now that I know you're here, I'll make you a nice little treat from back home with a bit of spice in it, for tomorrow. . . . That'll do you more good than all the medicines they'll give you. And what's your name now?'

'Suzette. At home they call me Zetou.'

'Right, Zetou, see you tomorrow.'

She winked at me as she left.

I finally took a look at my tray; there was a plate of soup, a slice of ham with some mashed potatoes and a portion of cream cheese.

I had to make an enormous effort to swallow a mouthful of the soup, which wasn't salty enough for me;

the cream cheese was served without sugar. If it hadn't been twenty-four hours since I'd last eaten anything, I'd never have been able to get a meal like that down.

The small dark-haired girl from the row opposite came to collect my tray which she piled with the others on the table. I took the opportunity to ask her name and find out where the toilet was.

'My name's Monique. You want to go to the bog?'

I stared at her, once again faced with a word I didn't understand. Monique took my arm and led me to the right place. There were five W.C.s, the same number of washbasins and two bathtubs. None of the doors had locks. I splashed some water on my face; I'd have liked to have a shower. Monique told me there were no showers and you had to have Sister Melin's permission to have a bath, as we had to be supervised by a nurse. In any case there were no taps on the baths. You had to use a special key to turn on the water. I began to wonder what kind of a hospital I was in. Instead of going back to bed I made the most of the fact that I had got my balance back to go and see Sister Melin. She had her office between our ward and that of the younger girls. She wasn't there but there were two other nurses that I didn't know; one was writing and the other knitting.

'Please, I. . . I. . . would like to see Sister Melin.'

'She's not here; do you need something?' asked the one who was knitting.

'I'd like to have a bath.'

'That's all right. I'll come and fetch you before supper.'

'I'd like to write to my family; what's the address here?'

'Oh! All you have to do is to give us the letter and we'll send it on.'

I felt even more suspicious now.

After a moment's hesitation I plucked up my courage and blurted out, 'What kind of a hospital is this? It's not a lunatic asylum, I hope?'

'Oh! this is a perfectly normal hospital. This part is the Pierre Cousin Wing of the Charity Hospital. It's a special wing for children with particular problems, that's to say, socio-psychological difficulties. It's got nothing to do with lunatics.'

This talk of a special 'socio-psychological wing' didn't make me much the wiser, if at all. If I was going to get a better understanding of things I'd have to go about with a dictionary in my pocket. It seemed to me that we were a long way from the good 'French as spoken in France' that Mrs Paule had drummed into us with a stick. What with Monique's vocabulary and 'socio-psychology', I was completely lost. When I spoke Creole, words had no mystery for me; it was really my own language. However, Mrs Paule used to forbid us to speak Creole at school, even during playtime.

Why? That's another question I shall have to find an answer to one day. . . .

I went back to the big ward. It was time for the afternoon rest. Sarah smiled at me and went on reading. The girl on my right was staring at the ceiling as if she was afraid it would fall on her nose. Monique was sitting at the big table, writing. The others were asleep or were daydreaming of the world we had left when we entered this ward. I too climbed back into bed, anxious to get back to my ghosts: my island, the village, my little school problems that I thought I would solve by coming to Paris.

I was fifteen and I had just started standard six, determined to pass my primary certificate exam, the key to admission to the big school in town. My two brothers had both left school the previous June, having no interest in studying. Jose, at fourteen, was big for his age; he and father were as alike as two halves of the same calabash. By one of the chances of cross-breeding, he was the only one of us four children not to have frizzy hair, although he was the darkest-skinned. He worked for Mr Felix and dreamed of becoming a driver; but until he reached the age when he could get a licence he had to be content with loading the luggage on the roof of the bus, and keeping an eye on it.

Louis had just turned thirteen. He lived only for the sea. When I think how hard we had to shake him to get him out of bed in the morning in time for school! Once he became a fisherman, our Louis was the first up and he could be heard in the early hours of the morning going off whistling merrily.

Father never bothered about what Zelia and I did in class. He had little sympathy for education; he couldn't see the use of it. Since he left school he had never needed to write a letter or read a book or a magazine; and the only newspapers we ever received were those that had been used to wrap things in.

I loved to read and was greedy to learn new things. Besides my school books I possessed a dozen dusty paperback novels, kept in an old trunk, the only memento of our mother. I read and re-read these old books, whose yellowing pages were half eaten away by the thousands of cockroaches that lived permanently in the trunk.

All this reading was the despair of Grandma, who thought it was these books that had been responsible for making Mother dissatisfied with her own home. As far as Grandma was concerned, a girl never learnt anything useful out of a book. 'What does a girl need to know? How to cook, mend and keep the house clean,' she used to say.

I saw a different future for myself. I hoped against hope to get my primary certificate and be able to go to the big school in town and later on have a career.

Charles, Mr Felix's son, had been at this big school for two years now. He told me the exciting things he was learning and which were full of magic for me: mythology, physics, mathematics; and this had got nothing to do with our arithmetic problems about leaking taps and trains passing each other, especially when you've never seen a train or used a tap, as was the case with me.

There was a big library in town where Charles used to borrow books. One day he gave me one to read which was to mark a real turning point in my life, as it answered a certain number of questions I had been asking myself as long as I could remember.

It was a fairly important volume on the history and origins of the people of our island. Contrary to what I had been taught up till then, I discovered that our ancestors were not only the Gauls, but Negroes, snatched from their own country in the Gulf of Guinea, in Angola, Cape-Verde, Senegal, etc., and brought as prisoners to our island. The chapter on the material conditions of the slaves described the unthinkable tortures and punishments inflicted on them. I also read about their revolts on different islands and the support they gained for their cause from various white people who realised they were human beings and finally, the great day of liberation, on 27 April 1848. . . . I had already heard of Victor Schoelcher, of the abolition of slavery, but I had never felt that it had anything to do with me. In spite of my doubts about my origins, I had finally accepted that our ancestors were Gauls, and consequently that these Negroes who had been freed belonged to a race that had become extinct in the Dark Ages. At least that was the state of my knowledge when the contents of this book hit me like a punch in the chest, nearly knocking me off my balance.

Glorying in my new-found knowledge, I went triumphantly up to Mrs Paule a few days later, during the morning break.

She usually stayed in the classroom to correct our exercises, munching crumbly little biscuits with a nice smell that made our mouths water. That day she was munching her biscuits and turning over the pages of a magazine. I went up to her, very sure of myself, and as soon as she looked up from her reading, I said in a firm voice, very proud of my discovery, 'Mrs Paule, Charles has lent me a book that says our ancestors were black men, slaves that came from Africa.'

'Your ancestors, perhaps, not mine! Get out!' she screamed, just about choking with fury.

I didn't wait to be told twice and scuttled off to the playground, completely flabbergasted. Mrs Paule was a big stout Mulatto with a nose so flat it looked as though her mother had sat on it when she was born, and with thick lips and very crinkly hair. I couldn't believe that her ancestors had simply been Gauls. . . . I thought the incident closed when, just as we were leaving at lunch time, Mrs Paule told me to stay behind. When the other pupils had gone she said, 'Now! You'll come back at half past two with your father.'

'But, please teacher. . . !'

'I said half past two with your father!'

Without another word she waddled off, enveloped in her fat which showed through the skin of her forearms like deposits of curd.

She knew quite well that my father was somewhere out at sea and that the fishermen never returned before four o'clock!

Grandma wasn't in the village either. On Fridays she came back late from her allotment, crushed beneath the weight of her enormous basket of vegetables that she would go to sell the following day in the market.

I walked back home along the beach. A pig was snuffling in the sand under a sea-grape bush, digging for crabs.

I picked a bunch of sea-grapes for him and he ate them grunting with pleasure. Then he went off to sniff at an empty tin can that had been washed up by a wave.

I scanned the horizon, imagining that by some miracle Father might have had an unusually good catch and be coming home early . . . and I followed the track of a little cloud that looked exactly like Father John with his long grey beard. I arrived home having completely forgotten that it was my turn to cook the lunch that day. I found Zelia very annoyed at having to do me a favour that I would never have done her, as cooking was one of the many jobs that I hated. On the other hand I was quite happy to do the washing on Thursdays.

We would go off to the river Corossol, a merry band of women and children, with our bundles of washing on our heads. There we would laugh and sing as we scrubbed our washing on the stones. When we had finished, we went in for a dip ourselves, rubbing our bodies with a mixture of leaves: patchouli and indiawood leaves that left our skin sweet-smelling.

Some of us shampooed our hair with the remains of the laundry-soap and then made a rinse from an infusion of prickly pears that we crushed between two stones. This made our hair very manageable so that even the finest comb wouldn't get tangled up in it. The evening before that particular day I had swapped my turn to do the cooking for an extra laundry session. So my poor sister had to fill the pot two days running, in addition to her own week's cooking.

We ate without exchanging a word. I didn't dare say anything for fear of making things worse. Zelia left for school. I found myself quite alone and at a loose end, not knowing what to do to fill the two hours' wait till Father returned.

I walked automatically towards the path behind our house that led to the river. It was a serene afternoon, with the sun sinking slowly from the zenith towards the west. A slight breeze swayed the tops of the trees. 'You are the trees of life,' it whispered to the breadfruit tree and the coconut palm; 'thanks to you, men down there can eat and drink, clothe themselves and shelter from the arrows of the sun.' And it lingered a little longer among the fronds of the palms which danced for joy. 'And you, mancheneel tree, even your shade is deadly. . . . How many innocent victims have you taken this year with your little apples that you drop maliciously on the path?' The haughty mancheneel tree scarcely quivered at the idea of these crimes and the little breeze went on its way up to the wild bracken on the mountainside. The air was fragrant; the scent of freshly gathered incense floated below the sweet smell of the ylang-ylang.

The river told the pebbles all it had seen and done high up on the mountain and in the hamlet of Corossol.

I lay down on an enormous flat rock that stood in the middle of the river. I was carried back to the time when I was a little child of four or five, lying in the bottom of a boat.

I had gone out fishing with Father; suddenly tired and frightened by the immense stretches of water all around us, I had lain down in the bottom of the boat so that I could see nothing but the sky and Father's reassuring back.

Had this scene really taken place? I recalled it every time some unexpected event occurred in my life, such as the night following Mother's departure, and one day when a violent tempest blew up while Father was at sea. On each occasion I found refuge from my anxiety in the bottom of a boat.

It was well past two o'clock when I woke up on my rock, with my sides quite stiff and bruised. I walked downstream to the sea, then along the beach as far as the creek where the fishermen beached their craft, and there I waited for Father. To try my patience, Father's boat, *By God's Grace*, came in the very last and I had to wait for the end of the sharing out, and for all the discussions and sales to be finished before I could reveal my problem to him.

'Why have I got to go and see Mrs Paule?' he asked in astonishment.

'Perhaps it's about the exam,' I said.

I could have given him any other answer! To tell the truth, I couldn't see any link between a book and Mrs Paule's anger.

Mrs Paule used to chuck us out of her class for all sorts of trivial reasons: for fighting in class, for running away when she beat us over the head and shoulders with her cane, or for not learning our lessons properly. But to think that she might expel me for reading a book, even if it wasn't to her taste – no, really! I let Father confront her alone. The discussion lasted a few minutes that seemed very long to me.

'Mrs Paule says that you were impertinent and that you'll be no better off with your primary certificate and you're old enough to look after the house.'

I was struck speechless with astonishment. Father, for his part, was not in the least upset, as he was opposed to my plan to continue my education after the primary certificate. If I went off to town, according to him, I would be 'lost'. How can anyone get lost in a town? I could understand getting lost in an isolated place, like on the mountain, where there was nobody to tell you the way. The idea of staying at home all alone for days on end gave me courage: I decided to do everything possible to make Mrs Paule go back on her decision. But what could I do? I had no idea. So I went to the shop to wait for Mr Felix and Charles to come back so that I could ask their advice.

Mr Felix was in Mrs Paule's good books. According to some people there had been something of a romance between them ten years previously, when Mrs Paule first arrived from another island to replace the old teacher who had taught my father the ABC and prepared my mother for the primary certificate.

'Well, well, Zetou, it's you, dearie! Have you come to wait for your sweetheart?'

Mrs Felix had long had plans for me. She saw me married to their only son. The fact was that we were always together. All the inhabitants of our village, without exception, were waiting for us to be old enough to go through the usual formalities. Charles and I had more or less the same plans for our future. He wanted to become a doctor and I a schoolteacher. He thought I ought rather to train to be a nurse so that we could work together. But the idea of looking after other people's aches and pains or giving injections was enough to make me feel ill. The sight of blood, even from a little scratch, made me faint.

One evening Jose had rushed into the house from the veranda. He had hurt himself and was holding his right hand which he placed under the light of the paraffin lamp standing on the table. I was carefully copying out a recitation. At that moment a drop of blood fell on the sheet of paper. I shuddered and right through that night thousands of closely packed bloodstained pages streamed past me as soon as I closed my eyes. . . .

For a moment my courage forsook me; I burst into tears and between my sobs stammered out my incoherent story of how I had been expelled from school.

'What!' Mrs Felix roared, calling on all her customers

as witness. 'I always said that that foreign female was crazy. She does her best to hold our youngsters back and then chucks them out of school for absolute trifles. You hear that! A kid who works so hard! She won't get away with it, I can tell you!'

Mrs Felix looked really furious, and the idea of using this opportunity of getting even with Mrs Paule for an old debt might possibly have had something to do with her anger.

'Don't cry, Zetou. Come and help me instead; go and fill Mrs Mano's bottle with paraffin.'

Then she resumed her monologue. She loved to talk. Like her husband and son she always had something new to tell.

A moment later the bus arrived.

'Hi, everyone!' Mr Felix shouted cheerfully as he jumped out.

'It's about time! Come and see what you can do for Zetou before you go off for your rum,' his wife replied.

'Hold on, woman! Give me a chance; I've scarcely got home. There's not a tidal wave, eh?'

'No! It's worse than that. . . .'

'Well now, Zetou, what're you in such a state about, eh? You haven't drowned your old dad, as far as I know!'

Mr Felix, still joking, took my hand and led me to one side. Charles approached and I told both of them the cause of my trouble.

'Well, yes, I'd better go and see her straightaway. I can't promise you anything. Sometimes it's as hard to get anything into that Mrs Paule's head as into all the coconuts round here,' Mr Felix said.

'Don't worry now,' Charles consoled me. 'You'll see, Dad'll settle the whole matter. . . . And besides, even if you don't go on with your studies, it won't matter – you can look after the children as we'll have lots of children.'

'Don't be so stupid! There's a heap of things I want to do before I get married. I shan't learn them here in the village.'

Far from consoling me, the idea of having nothing but housework and children to occupy my time later was most depressing. If any man in the village knew the little interest I took in all domestic work there's no doubt he'd exclaim, 'That girl takes after her mother; she'll come to no good, we shall lose her one day!'

After he'd been away for a good half hour, Mr Felix came back whistling.

'Good! That's it, she'll take you back. But the first time you get on the wrong side of her, you'll be selling your father's fish. That's your future as far as Mrs Paule's concerned. And it's going to cost me two good hours of errands I've got to do for her in town tomorrow.'

I was sweating. The central heating was on and I had a woollen blanket over me. The ward was bustling with activity. The 'knitting nurse' was distributing thermometers.

'You know where to put it?'

'Yes.'

Of course I knew where to put it. Although my case history said I couldn't adapt to life in France, the thermometer is an instrument of civilisation that already existed on our island. It's true, we didn't own one. On the rare occasions that one of us was ill, Grandma borrowed one from Mrs Felix.

'Let's see. You've got a bit of a temperature, nearly 101. Any aches or pains?'

'My throat's rather sore.'

She looked at my throat, depressing my tongue with a thin strip of wood.

'It's nothing much; your throat's a bit inflamed. I'll give you something for it in a bit.'

'And my bath?'

'Not today, I'm afraid now.'

'That's just my luck. I feel so dirty. . . .'

It was the first time I'd ever had an inflamed throat. This country really didn't suit me. The other girls were sitting on their beds. The girl on my left, Sarah, was doing her hair, with a mirror in one hand and a comb in the other, and humming a popular tune, 'Paloma'.

The girl on my right didn't seem very talkative; I

hadn't heard her voice all day. She kept her hooked nose buried in her book and looked surly. Her brown hair was cut very short and stuck out stiffly like the fronds of a coconut palm. She wore glasses and her face was pimply. I didn't feel much attracted to her, nevertheless I made a move to start a conversation as soon as she got off her bed.

'What's your name? I'm Suzette.'

She glanced at me in annoyance and murmured 'Helen!' as she made her way to the toilet. This girl aroused my curiosity and I took the chance while she was out of the room to ask Sarah about her.

'I say, Sarah, d'you know what's wrong with Helen? She looks so disagreeable.'

Sarah first looked round to make sure Helen wasn't within earshot.

'She pushed her little brother into the river and he drowned. Her mother always took the brother's side against her; he was the favourite. She's going on trial and. . . .'

'Did she tell you that herself?'

'No, of course not. Monique told me. Monique knows everything that happens; she's been here for three or four years.'

'Four years! That's impossible!'

To spend four years wandering round a bed in a hospital ward for a girl who looked quite healthy. . . . And there was I wondering how I could manage to hold out for a week without going completely out of my mind. . . .

I had forgotten that when Sarah started talking it was like a tap that couldn't be turned off, or a bubbling spring that couldn't be stopped. So she went on, 'Monique is an orphan. She was ill-treated by the family she lived with and they brought her here because she suffered from insomnia. Since then nobody has claimed her. She's sort of adopted by the nurses; she has access to Sister Melin's office and she sees all the case histories and hears what they say about each of us.'

Monique occupied bed number 6, immediately opposite the girl on my right. Beds 4 and 8 opposite me were empty, as two girls had gone home that morning.

Bed number 2 belonged to a tall fair-haired girl – the one who had called 'Look out!' to warn us of the doctors' arrival. She was only fourteen. She had a face like a full moon, very pale blue eyes and a terrible accent. She was from Alsace. She'd had a baby by her father.

Now that my curiosity was aroused, Sarah did not have to be asked twice to give me all the details of all the other girls' cases.

Bed number 10, opposite Sarah, was occupied by a mysterious girl, Irene. With all her shrewdness, Monique had not been able to discover where she came from or why she was here. As far as could be seen, she wasn't having any treatment. She was thought not to speak French as she smiled at everything anyone said to her and never replied.

Perhaps she was Italian or Spanish with her velvety black eyes and long jet-black hair. But her quiet, gentle manner might mean that she was badly mentally retarded. The first bed on my side was occupied by Colette, a small, shrivelled, nervy girl. She jerked about all the time and tugged at a lock of hair that hung over her bony face. She lived on an isolated farm in the Aisne Department, near Laon. One evening, when she came home from school, she had found her father hanging from a beam in the barn. She ran away and wandered all night in the woods. For the last three months, she had not uttered a single intelligible sentence, except, 'It's impossible!' She'd just had three weeks of shock treatment, but her condition didn't seem to have improved; it could even have got worse, as now she screamed out at night.

As for number 3, she had just turned thirteen. She had tried to commit suicide after her parents' divorce and had taken an overdose of sleeping pills. Fortunately, her mother had come home earlier than expected and she had been saved. The shock treatment was doing her good; after two months she had got back her interest in life and she sometimes sang to herself quite cheerfully.

I was completely shattered by the descriptions Sarah had just given me of our fellow-patients.

According to the 'knitting nurse', this wasn't a lunatic asylum, so there couldn't be any mad people in this ward. But, in fact, weren't we all even more wretched than people who can take refuge in madness?

To spend months and years in bed, without having anything physically wrong with you, at an age when other youngsters were running wild in the country, going to school, making plans for the future! What 'socio-psychological' future could we look forward to? And that's civilisation! Shutting up children who need sunlight, pure air and, above all, affection! I'd prefer never to adapt to this civilisation. Out of the eight girls in our ward, not one had had a normal family life. Sarah, who besides her blackouts seemed perfectly stable, had lost her father, who had been killed by the Germans in the 1939–45 war. And because she was Jewish, part of her childhood had been spent in a cellar infested with rats. It was after this period in the cellar that her blackouts began.

I could reckon myself lucky as, in spite of my mother's leaving us, my childhood had been the same as that of all the children in our village. I had grown up in the country, surrounded by sea and sun. Today, I would like to draw from my past the strength to face the present. Will this be possible?

Monique, who had just come back from the nurses' office, told us that it was snowing.

'Snow! I'd love to see it; I've never seen snow!'

'Really!' said Monique, very surprised. 'Wait, I'll go and ask Sister Melin. . . .'

She came back a few minutes later.

'Come. She'll let you look out of her office window. You can't go outside with a sore throat.'

It was better than nothing. I'd have liked to touch this snow. . . . Guessing my thoughts Sister Melin said, 'If your temperature's down tomorrow, you can touch it when we go to see Dr Edward.'

'Perhaps it will have gone by tomorrow,' I said, my

disappointment sounding in my voice.

'It's the first snow of the season in Paris. You'll have other opportunities, you know. . . .'

'Yes, of course. . . .'

Still, I was very disappointed. To see snow from behind a pane of glass, from the warmth of a room, was no different from what I had already seen at the cinema in a film about mountain rescues.

When I got back to the ward, Doudou was there, pushing her trolley. Monique went to give out the trays. I took mine and sat down at the table rather than going back to bed. The evening meal was no better than the lunch. A slice of cold meat instead of the ham, and a spoonful of jam instead of the cream cheese. For the rest, the remains of the midday meal had probably gone into the unsalted soup.

A bit later the 'knitting nurse' came round with tablets for those who had to take them and then switched off the lights. It was barely half past six. Only a little blue bulb above the door to the lavatories shed a faint light in which I could distinguish Sarah's delicate features.

She was not asleep and was certainly thinking of something funny as a faint smile played round her lips.

After resting all day I was not sleepy. I no longer felt angry and could begin to judge the absurd cruelty of the world I had entered the day I left Father's house.

'It's always too late to say, "If only I'd known"' is a saying with us.

What would I not give, in fact, to be able to wipe out this whole month in Paris and take up my life on the island that I had left one autumn morning! My problems with Mrs Paule were just a flash in the pan compared to the thunderbolt that had consumed my innocence in four weeks. . . .

If you take into account the five hours' time difference, it's half past one in the afternoon in Cocotier. Zelia must be getting ready to go back to school. After I left, Father had let her return. How I envied her her peaceful, well-ordered life! I shall never know that peace again, even if I go back to live in Cocotier. I have lost that pure vision of things that one glimpses through the veil of innocence. Today, by concentrating all my thoughts on recalling the past, I hope to delay as long as possible the moment when I shall have to think about the present which I find so confusing. So, once again I closed my eyes to resume my dream. Cocotier.

The day after Mr Felix's intervention, I went back to school as usual. Mrs Paule ignored me. That didn't worry me in the slightest; all I wanted was to pass my exam at the end of the year. . . .

On Saturday afternoons Mrs Paule let us out half an hour early. Zelia and I rushed home and set off immediately to go for a swim in the river Corossol. A merry party of children were splashing about in the pool.

I washed my hair and then rinsed it with the prickly-pear infusion, and Zelia tied it in curling rags so that I would have curls for Mass the following day. Then we walked upstream with two schoolfriends, Laurence and Marie, to fill our water-bottles with drinking water, a long way up from the pool and the places where we usually did our washing.

The Corossol was not much more than six feet wide where we stopped. The water was unbelievably cold and clear; on the banks 'pink apples' and wild peas grew in abundance. We sat down for a while to eat some on the spot. Then we ran back to the beach again. A few fishing-boats were coming in. The last rays of the setting sun were reflected in thousands of tiny copper-coloured flakes, turning the horizon red.

Father and Louis came back a little later than usual, their wide-brimmed hats pushed to the backs of their heads, their faces drawn. The catch had not been good, the sea was rough. A few small fish squirmed in the bottom of the boat. But we were in seventh heaven as Louis had caught a *chatou*, a shell-fish like a large lobster. We would have it for Sunday lunch cooked with rice and it would be a change from our daily diet of sweet potatoes with cod, or fish soup.

The next morning we were up early, as on every

Sunday, so as to clean up the house a bit and prepare lunch before leaving for church. It was an absolute duty to go to Mass every Sunday. Father John was always saying it was a mortal sin to miss Mass unless one were seriously ill. So the whole village and the surrounding hamlets flocked to fill Cocotier's little Saint Sophie's Church, the only brick building in the village. It also served as a shelter in the event of a cyclone or a tidal wave. The men in their heavily starched white duck trousers arrived in a chorus of 'plop! plop!'. The women, for the most part, wore long dresses of flowered cotton and funny straw hats with bunches of fruit, flowers and all sorts of ribbons, or else cotton headscarves.

Father John wouldn't let any women or girls into church without some sort of head covering. The Mass was always too long. Father John would go on and on, exhorting us to chastity, goodness, charity and many other virtues. He could see sin everywhere. Knowing, as all the inhabitants of Cocotier did, that I spent most of my leisure hours almost exclusively with Charles, he once asked me during confession, 'Has Charles ever touched you, my child?' When I looked uncomprehending, he said, 'Never let him see what you've got between your thighs, and much less touch you there; it would be a mortal sin.' I felt terribly ashamed. He must have asked Charles the same question, but I never heard anything more about it. . . .

It was beautiful weather that Sunday, contrary to the forecast. The sky was quite clear. When we came out of the dim, cool church at eleven o'clock, the sun was quite dazzling. For once the idea of the succulent dish of rice and *chatou* sent us straight home, instead of dawdling for long outside the church. It's true that we never had anything to eat before Mass as we had to take communion on an empty stomach. . . .

In Cocotier nobody ever locked their doors, even if they had a lock on them. No one would ever think of entering a house when the occupants were out. One would just wait on the veranda till they came back. When we went out we used to put a big stone up against the front door; that was the way everyone shut up their houses.

When we got as far as the Felixes' we were astonished to see the stone moved and the door open. Someone was in our house. Not one of the inhabitants of the village, nor any of the surrounding hamlets; but perhaps it was an animal . . . and suppose it had eaten our *chatou*. . . . Without a word we started to walk faster and Louis and Jose broke into a run. When they reached the front door they stopped as if turned to stone, hesitated a moment, then went in. Zelia and I followed behind Father and Grandma, as we weren't very brave in circumstances like this.

As I reached the veranda I heard a woman's voice. A voice that I had not completely forgotten.

'Oh! How you've grown, Jose!'

My heart started to dance a frenzied *gros ka*. I recognised her immediately. . . .

She was even more beautiful than I had remembered. She looked like one of the ladies in fashion magazines. Her eyebrows were replaced by a pencil line, her lips and cheeks were made up. Her hair was drawn back to form an imposing chignon in the nape of her neck. She smiled. A cigarette was burning out in a plate that she had taken to use as an ashtray. Her white dress with little blue polka-dots was made out of a silky material with hundreds of tiny pleats in the skirt. She was wearing white shoes with heels so sharp that I wondered how anyone could really stand perched on them. The whole room was pervaded by a discreet but clinging perfume that was nothing like the cheap toilet waters we used on Sundays. It was as though a dazzling sunbeam were sitting there on the only decent chair that we still possessed, making everything look wretched and poverty-stricken in a way I had never noticed till then.

'Why now, my little Zetou, don't you recognise me? I'm your mother!'

I went up to her to kiss her. In spite of the smile on her face, her expression was quite different from the rest of her appearance; it was cold and almost contemptuous.

She had come back just as she had left six years ago, without any warning, once more upsetting the peaceful, regular rhythm of our simple life as a fisherman's children. Father, after a brief greeting, as if to someone he had left five minutes earlier, went off to the bar, probably to drown in rum the memory of his flouted love.

Jose, Louis, Zelia and I were too intimidated by this beautiful lady to say a word. Grandma was in ecstasies of joy at her daughter's return and asked her a thousand and one questions.

'What do you intend to do now?' she asked.

'I'm thinking of staying in town for two or three months to see about my divorce.'

'Divorce!' cried Grandma.

'Yes, I want to be free, you understand?'

'Oh well . . . I thought you were going to stay with us now. . . . Well, I'll go and see about lunch.'

Grandma was clearly very disappointed. She must have thought that like the 'prodigal son' in one of Father John's sermons, her child had returned, repentant.

When Grandma went out Mother turned to me.

'How are you getting on at school, Zetou?'

'Er . . . all right.'

'What class are you in?'

'Standard six.'

'Is that all! You're very behindhand. In France children of fifteen have already passed their School Certificate. And you haven't even got your primary certificate, have you? . . . It's true your father doesn't think education is of much use. I suppose he hasn't done anything to encourage you to study.'

'I've never been kept down a year,' I said.

She had forgotten that she had sent me to school very late, at eight and a half instead of at six, and that it had taken me a year to learn French. Like all the village children I had spoken Creole until I started school.

'And you, Jose, you're getting on all right?'

'Me! Oh, I'm all right!'

Jose, obviously too embarrassed to admit that he

didn't go to school any more, after Mother's outcry on the subject, dashed out of the house. Zelia, who was not very talkative by nature, slipped away discreetly, to avoid any awkward questions.

Louis was fairly shy; nevertheless, he had no complexes; in fact he was rather proud of his job as a fisherman. Anticipating Mother's question, he said, 'I've left school. I help Father with the fishing.'

'You're going to become a fisherman, then!' she said, in a voice that clearly indicated that she meant 'What a disgrace!'

'Mother, I want to go on studying after my primary certificate. Take me back to Paris with you.'

I blurted this out rapidly, without thinking.

'We'll see. . . . You're already old enough for secondary school. . . . Look,' she went on, pointing to a box on the table. 'Open it. I've brought some little presents for you.'

Then she took out her packet of cigarettes. They were Players. The only brand of cigarettes you could buy in Cocotier were called 'Jobs'. But most men smoked a pipe or rolled their own cigarettes with the thin papers that they bought from Mrs Felix. Normally I didn't like the smell of tobacco, but the smoke from the Players was like a real perfume, and I enjoyed sniffing it.

Louis got to the box first and opened it. There were clothes for all of us, including a shirt for Father. The dress intended for me was far too big. The fact is that at fifteen and a half I was small for my age. I was slender rather than thin, and quite strong.

The people in the village used to say that I took after my mother and that I was pretty like her. I didn't think I was beautiful, not even pretty, or even at all nice-looking. It's true I had my mother's big eyes, but my lips were thicker, my mouth bigger, my nose too large for my face and my front teeth decayed. I had never been to a dentist; whenever I'd had toothache it had been treated with cloves put into the cavity, which gave my breath a spicy smell.

Mother had healthy, even, white teeth. Her smile

could have been used as an advertisement for some brand of toothpaste. . . .

Grandma had surpassed herself. The rice with *chatou* was delicious and Mother did our cooking the honour of taking a second helping. Grandma even found a few pence to buy us some iced lemonade from Mrs Felix.

At about three o'clock a black Peugeot 203 stopped in front of our house. It was Mr Milan. Mother left, promising to come and see us again while she was still in town. Father came in after supper. He had reverted to silence and did not answer when I asked him what he had been doing all day.

The next morning we all resumed our normal activities. School with Mrs Paule didn't bring me much satisfaction. I couldn't see how my school year was going to end. She was quite capable of refusing to enter me for the exam. She had taken me back, contrary to her custom, to do Mr Felix a favour. She never addressed a word to me, never asked me any questions in class. However, she did correct my exercises.

Mother did not come back to see us as she had promised. But she saw Grandma every Saturday at the market in town. Six weeks after she had turned up in Cocotier, she got her divorce without any difficulty, and under all the conditions that she had asked for. They had been married under community of property, but she let Father keep everything, not out of generosity, but simply because she had no use for a fishing-boat and a wooden hut – Father's sole possessions. She obtained custody of Zelia and myself, although she had no wish to take us away with her. We were to remain with Grandma. Mother's lawyer was a white man from town, a friend of Mr Milan. Father didn't engage a lawyer. He went off twice in Mr Felix's bus at six in the morning to attend the court hearings in town.

Having always associated his domestic troubles with too much schooling, Father decided to keep Zelia and me at home now, for fear of losing us too. He went to let Mrs Paule know and she was quite pleased since, as far as she was concerned, fisherfolk's children didn't need to know anything except the three Rs. Then he announced after supper that the next day Zelia and I were to go off to help Grandma in the fields.

'What!' I shouted. 'I want to go on with my education!'

My left cheek smarted from the resounding slap I received. It was the very first time Father had ever struck me. I fled, more surprised than angry. . . .

The beach was deserted, the sand still warm, the sky sprinkled with twinkling stars. I sat down for a moment to try to see clearly into my own mind. I understood my poor father's reaction, nevertheless I was determined not to give in. Later on he would be only too pleased to have an educated daughter when he was too old to spend all day out at sea, waiting for the fish to bite, or pulling on a net that comes up empty more often than not. I couldn't understand how Zelia could accept Father's decision without a word. I couldn't understand how she could put up with everything with the same equanimity. . . .

A shooting star! I just had time to make a wish before it disappeared. . . .

Suddenly I remembered that Mother had not said no when I asked her to take me to Paris. I went home and wrote her a letter, asking her to help me; she was my only hope now. The next morning I went to Mr Felix's as he was leaving at six o'clock and gave my letter to Charles who knew where Mother was staying, telling him of this new nasty blow. I asked him to insist on Mother giving him an answer immediately, and in any case before she left town, which couldn't be very long now.

Mother took three days to think about it. I learnt some time later that it was Mr Milan who advised her to take me, saying that after all it was her duty as she had obtained custody of her daughters. So, three days after I had written my letter, I received a reply that surpassed all my hopes, as I had never imagined that Mother would decide to take me back with her straightaway. There was a five-franc note in the envelope and a few lines telling me to send three photos and my birth certificate so that she could get me a passport. . . .

Grandma was delighted that I was going with her daughter. I left her the responsibility of telling Father, whom I didn't dare confront since he had slapped my face.

Zelia was completely opposed to my leaving. She thought it was quite unwise for me to set off on this unknown venture. 'You know what you're leaving behind, you don't know what you'll find over there.' She wouldn't leave her village for anything in the world. Her ambitions went no further than the village of Cocotier, even the nearby town didn't attract her, as it was too noisy. I thought that Zelia was a little fool. What danger could I run? None at all. In Paris my future was assured; all I had to do was to settle down seriously to my school work; my future depended on myself, and so it was quite assured.

Two days after receiving Mother's letter I went off to town in Mr Felix's bus. Jose took me to a photographer who specialised in passport photos. Then I went to the hotel where Mother was staying. It was in the square from which the buses left for the different villages and regions of the island. I didn't know what name Mother was going under, so I asked for Mr Milan. Without taking his nose out of his newspaper, the grey-haired old white man, who must have been the proprietor of the hotel, replied that he was out.

'And the lady with him?'

'She's out.'

'Can I wait for them?' I asked, more and more intimidated by this man who looked just like the polar bear in my reading book, with his hairy arms and mop of white hair.

'Please yourself.'

Finally I decided to go and wait for them outside. I didn't feel at ease sitting opposite this man who seemed so starved for news that he was devouring his paper rather than reading it.

After a good half hour, during which I could have gone for a tour round the island in one of the multi-coloured buses that were arriving and departing from the square, I caught sight of Mother coming back alone.

She was wearing trousers and low-heeled shoes. She didn't look like the lady I'd seen six weeks before at Cocotier; her hair was short, whereas I'd seen her at our house with a large bun, which gave the impression that she had long hair. Naturally I knew nothing at that time about how one could change one's appearance with wigs and false pieces. As for the trousers, it was the first time I'd seen a woman dressed like that.

She greeted me quite pleasantly, but without warmth.

'Well! How are you, Zetou? Have you got the papers and the passport photos?'

'Yes, Mother.'

'Right then, give them to me. Roger' (she meant Mr Milan) 'will see about your passport. He's got friends at the prefecture; it won't take long. . . . You'll have to have a smallpox vaccination . . . and . . . only take what you'll need on the boat. I'll buy you some decent clothes in Paris. We'll be leaving early next Tuesday, that's in one week's time exactly. You can sleep here on Monday night. Well, I must leave you, I've got a lot to do before lunch.'

She left me standing there on the pavement and disappeared into the hotel. I couldn't go back to Cocotier before evening and anyway Mr Felix's bus was no longer in the square. I didn't dare wander off by myself as I didn't know my way about in town. Besides, I didn't know where to go for this vaccination. After several minutes' hesitation I plucked up all my courage and went back into the hotel.

'I'd like to see Mr Milan's lady.'

'Number 6, first floor.'

The old polar bear was still buried in his newspaper. I went along a rather dark corridor and found a staircase right at the end. On the first floor I knocked at the door which bore the number indicated. As soon as Mother opened it I blurted out very quickly, for fear she could intimidate me, 'Excuse me, I don't know where to go for the vaccination and Mr Felix's bus isn't there any more. . . .'

'All right, come in. Roger won't be long. He'll show you where to go.'

The room, which was really quite simple, seemed luxurious to me as I'd never seen anything like it. It was large and harmoniously furnished with curtains and a bedcover of flowered cretonne, a table and two bamboo armchairs.

As far as the 'lot to do before lunch' was concerned, Mother was doing her long and carefully manicured nails. I felt ashamed as I watched her and crossed my arms, clenching my fists to hide my nails which were cut extremely short. We didn't exchange another word for the rest of the time until Roger arrived, which seemed an age to me. Finally he appeared, smiling and much more pleased to see me than my mother had been. He was sunburnt, with prominent cheekbones, grey-green eyes, golden-brown hair, an Adam's apple that bobbed up and down, and a genuinely warm smile.

'Hello! It's our little Zetou: Now, isn't she a little beauty! Of course we know who she takes after. . . .'

He took both my hands and planted a kiss on my forehead.

Mother smiled and a gleam of happiness appeared in her eyes; it must have been pleasure at Roger's return!

'Are you coming? I'm starving,' he said.

Then, taking each of us by the hand, he led Mother and me into the hotel restaurant where five or six tables, covered with red-checked tablecloths, were set out in the courtyard under a pergola of apple-creepers. I greedily gobbled up the mixed hors d'oeuvres, not realising that there would be two more courses to follow, taking no notice of Mother or Roger.

When I had wiped my plate clean I looked up, my hunger satisfied. Then I met my mother's cold angry gaze, while she said in a very sweet voice, 'You eat too fast, Zetou!'

Whether it was the effect of the look she gave me, or the excessive sweetness of her voice, or a combination of the two, I can't say, but I felt as though a huge lump were blocking my throat and I could swallow nothing more for the rest of the meal.

That evening, on the way back to Cocotier, Charles and I had a long discussion. He was very pleased with the way things had turned out.

'You're very lucky, and then when I get to Paris, after I've got my matric, I shan't be lost as you can show me around.'

'Of course,' I said, 'on one condition.'

'What's that?'

'That you write to me every day for the next four years, giving me all the news of the village, even the most harmless gossip.'

'Is that all! I don't make any promises; that's really asking a bit too much. One letter a week will be quite enough.'

'All right! Then you can look for another guide when you get to Paris.'

We burst out laughing noisily, waking a dried-up, bent old man who was a stranger to me, who had been dozing.

'That's right, young people can laugh at anything.'

'You're not going to get much sleep today, Gaffer Tison, with those two,' Mr Felix said to the old man.

'Mmm!' was his reply.

'That's Destinville's kid, the fisherman. She's going off to Paris next week with her mother. That's what they're all excited about.'

'Hm! That's nothing to rejoice about. Those towns aren't the place for us. I was there in 1918 for their war with the Germans. In a whole week I never saw the sun once and it was so cold that one day when I had to sweep the yard with a Senegalese, we started to cry like two little kids, our fingers were so stiff and sore with the cold; we couldn't hold the broom. Fortunately it was nearly the end of the war; we were sent to the south where it wasn't so cold. All those who went out at the beginning of the war died; not a single one came back to the island. Those that weren't killed by the Germans, the cold must have done for.'

Nobody believed a word of old Tison's rambling talk. Nevertheless we all listened in complete silence until he got out at Bananier, the little village before ours.

Father took things very well, at least outwardly. After his brief outburst, when he had hit me, he reverted to his taciturn habits. The news of my departure had spread rapidly through the village and the neighbouring hamlets. Many people came to see me; some of them brought me some little souvenir or other, according to their means. Unfortunately I had to leave the majority of their gifts behind: bags, shell-necklaces, fruit, among other things. Mother had insisted that I mustn't take anything useless. As far as she was concerned, nothing from Cocotier had any value. To avoid any temptation on my part, she had bought me the smallest possible suitcase.

Mrs Paule took the trouble to come and say goodbye to me the day before my departure. Now that I was going to live in Paris and go to school there, I was no longer simply a fisherman's daughter, good for nothing except sewing patches on the men's trousers. She gave me the address of her brother in Paris. I made a note of it, quite determined never to meet this brother.

When the last visitors had gone, it was half past ten. My brothers were chatting on the veranda with other boys and girls of their own age. Grandma then announced that we must set out for Corossol where we were to pay a visit to the sorcerer who would see if my journey was to take place under lucky omens.

Grandma took a chicken, a large yam, a candle and a little money to pay for the consultation.

It was a bright moonlit night. The cocks of the neighbourhood were paying their tribute to the silver moon in a noisy concert, to which the night birds added their cries and the rustle of their wings. We were lit on our way by a cheerful escort of fireflies. The ground was warm beneath our bare feet. A pleasant smell of freshly crushed grass mingled with the faint scent of the ylang-ylang. Oh! how pleasant my last night in Cocotier was . . .!

The sorcerer lived on the outskirts of Corossol. A tiny

footpath behind the hamlet led to a hut that came into sight some little way from the steep climb. A dog greeted us in quite a friendly fashion. He seemed to know us, preceded us to the hut and growled slightly as if to say, 'Here they are. . . .'

The man was smoking a long, crudely carved pipe. He was much younger than I had imagined a sorcerer to be. His sole garment was a piece of red material tied at his waist and he wore a necklace made of shells and the teeth of animals that I had never seen before.

'Ah! *Moune en moin! Moune en moin!* My people, my people!' the sorcerer said slowly. 'Is this the child who is going on a journey?'

'Yes, Papa Logbo,' Grandma replied.

Papa Logbo got up. Grandma took my hand and we followed him. The room we went into was smaller than the first one. Above the door was a wooden cross and opposite it was another cross drawn in white chalk in the middle of which was fixed a pair of scissors. Wooden statuettes stood on a table with rickety legs, projecting their shadows up to the roof of corrugated iron, from which hung a tangle of strings. At the end of each piece of string hung a bunch of leaves. The inside walls were covered with inscriptions and geometric drawings. An oil lamp made out of half a coconut shell cast a feeble light on a statue of Christ which stood on a shelf covered with a white cloth.

Papa Logbo sat down on the edge of a narrow bed covered with a jute cloth. He traced a cabalistic figure on the ground, composed of a double triangle that looked like a star. He wrote some letters and figures in it, then drew up a block of wood that served as a seat and made me sit on it. He lit the candle that Grandma had brought and gave it to me to hold. Still smoking his pipe he tapped the ground with his left foot. After a moment he gave a start, then began to snigger while he rocked backwards and forwards.

'Mamma Gastonia! Hee! hee! hee . . .! You ought to have come to see me sooner so that I could do something for the child. . . .'

'Yes?' said Grandma, very worried.

'*Enhan! Enhan!* I see good and bad. Our gods of Africa are not favourable for the immediate future. *Enhan! Enhan! Enhan!* I'll do what I can tonight. . . .'

Thereupon Papa Logbo left us and went out. After ten to fifteen minutes he came back carrying a large tub filled with a mixture of greenish water and leaves. He told me to undress and get into the tub. The water was warm and gave off an indefinable but pleasant smell. The sorcerer took the leaves and rubbed my body, while repeating incantations in a strange language – that of the gods of Africa, no doubt. Papa Logbo was really quite a nice person who knew where we came from and how to talk to the gods of Africa. I was so full of wonder that, forgetting my shyness, I asked him, 'Have you been to Africa, Papa Logbo?'

'Yes, my child. I go back there every day, several times a day, to consult our gods.'

After the bath, the sorcerer lit a charcoal fire in a clay pot. He poured a few drops of a liquid and various powders on to the fire, then made me step over this fire seven times.

'The river does not wash away what is meant for you.'

We had been at sea for two days, on one of the boats of the Transatlantic Company, sailing to Le Havre. Mother and Roger occupied a luxurious cabin in first class. I had a bed in the women's dormitory down in steerage. It was very stuffy and a lot of people were seasick. Fortunately I proved to be a good sailor and I could stay on deck the whole day. I hadn't seen Mother since we embarked. She had jotted down the number of her cabin; when I wanted to go there the steward that I asked the direction from told me that passengers from my class were not allowed there without permission from the captain. When I explained that my mother was in first class, he promised to ask her to come to fetch me or to send me a permit. In the afternoon Roger came for me about four o'clock. He could go anywhere on the boat, like all the first class passengers. Everyone greeted him and he seemed to know all the members of the crew as well as the passengers.

We joined Mother in one of the first class lounges. There were rows of luxuriously comfortable armchairs made of soft, creamy leather. The tables were made of a golden metal with glass tops; thick blue velvet curtains and huge tapestries covered part of the walls.

The rest of the walls were covered with fine carved panelling. Everything seemed very grand to me. I had never imagined such luxury.

One of the waiters came up to take our order. Mother asked for water-ices and orangeade for all three of us, without asking what we preferred. Roger lit a Players and passed it to Mother, then lit one for himself. Nobody spoke in this lounge. A pianist was playing a strangely sweet tune that induced a feeling of melancholy.

I put my foot in it for the first time by asking Mother who this music was by. She didn't reply, visibly very annoyed. Roger had not heard my question. I then kept quiet. I could feel that Mother was ashamed of me. I was also ashamed of my plain cotton dress, my cheap shoes – the only pair I possessed that I wore to go to Mass on Sundays, as in Cocotier no one bothered about shoes to go to school in.

I didn't fit in with the opulence of this room and the other people there. Fortunately my embarrassment didn't last long. I said to myself that I really couldn't care less if she was ashamed of me; that was her business, not mine. The important thing was that the water-ice was delicious. A pity my orangeade was not sweet enough. Clearly, if I asked for some sugar, Mother would choke with rage. Poor woman, I thought. She hadn't answered my question, as she probably didn't know much about music. But people mustn't guess this as a lady in her position was supposed to know everything. Or almost everything. I was beginning to understand her. . . .

As it happened, Rosamond (that was my mother's name) hadn't a clue what the piece of music was that she was hearing for the first time, and probably would never know. And to ask Roger, or anyone else, would show up the gaps in her own education. Oh, no! Never! That would never do. She seemed very depressed, no doubt this music suggested something which touched her, and that she couldn't put a name to.

'Oh Lord,' she must have been thinking, 'why haven't I ever felt any real affection for my children? It's true that I could never love their father, not really! He's too crude and primitive, and so black. . . . But the children take half after me, too. This little Zetou is really very sweet. I hope that I can grow a bit fond of her. I must make an attempt to, at least. . . .'

As for Roger, Rosamond gave him credit for far more knowledge than he did in fact have. He had learned to play the violin with more or less success. It was a tradition in his family: the boys played the violin, the girls the piano. He had no talent and had quickly given it up; he had preferred running about in the sun, in the company of the little piccanins on the estate, to the insipid Creole parties on the lawns or in shady drawing-rooms. Hunting with catapults, fishing, pilfering from the fields and listening to the funny stories that the little black kids told was much more fun, he found, than the squeaking sounds of a violin. Nevertheless, for once he enjoyed listening to this Chopin waltz which reminded him of his sister Francine. He used to hear her murdering this piece for months on end without ever managing to play it correctly.

Poor Francine had come to a tragic end. At eighteen she had been forced by her parents into the arms of a very rich young man from a neighbouring island, whom unfortunately she did not love. This boy had a great weakness for alcohol. One night Francine threw herself out of the window of the hotel bedroom where they were spending their honeymoon. It was not till the next morning, when he had slept off his rum, that the husband discovered what had happened. He was incapable of saying whether she had still been in the room when he had returned the previous night.

Sorrow, as much as age, had shortened the lives of their parents. So Roger found himself his own master at twenty-two. Taking life as it pleased him, he sponged on his brother when he had wasted away his own meagre inheritance.

He had not been a brilliant pupil at school. He had finally passed his School Certificate after a great deal of trouble and much extra tuition. He had already been aware of Rosamond's beauty when they had been together at high school. When he met her again, some years later, it had been love at first sight. On 14 July that year, he and two pals had decided to make the rounds of the little villages in search of new conquests. As soon as he got to Cocotier and recognised Rosamond, he decided to stay on there. His friends left. He spent the whole night dancing the beguine with Rosamond. He didn't have much difficulty in persuading her to come and live with him in town. She was wasting away in this village where nobody appreciated her; she was a generation in advance of all the other women.

'Dear, sweet Rosamond,' Roger must be saying to himself. 'I certainly adore her. She has the knack of inflaming my senses and my heart. There's no doubt she loves me. So she must have a heart. She's sensitive and usually quite generous, but she becomes impossible where her own family is concerned. And yet she owes her copper-coloured complexion and her exotic beauty to the half-Negro blood in her veins. It's that that bewitches me. I must admit the fisherman she was given as a husband was incapable of appreciating the choice morsel he had in his hands. Thank heaven for that! He didn't damage the goods too much by putting her four times in the family way. Zetou takes after her mother – she's full of character is this little miss. Her clothes make her look like a scarecrow. . . . I'll take her in hand when we get to Paris. If she's got what it takes we'll make something of her. . . .'

I was quite surprised to see Sister Melin, the sister-in-charge, arriving with the thermometers. It was quite dark outside. I could scarcely believe that a new day had begun. My night had been very short, as if I had dozed for only half an hour. My throat was still a little sore when I swallowed, but my temperature was normal. My present situation was nothing but a bad dream; when I woke up I would be back in my village. I would go for a long swim in the river, then lie on a flat rock in the middle of the stream. After that I'd go for a good walk as far as Raisin Clair and pick coco-plums and flowers to give to my friends.

I felt happy to be alive. I'll talk quite frankly to Dr Edward and he'll help me to return to my island. I'm sure he will help me. . . .

'Ah, ha! If you go back after what you've done, you'll be the laughing stock of the village. Charles isn't waiting for you. What young man will want to marry you? You're no longer worthy of them. That's where your foolish desire for more education has led you.'

'What? What did you say?'

'Nothing. . . .'

'Who spoke then?'

'Nobody,' Sarah replied.

'Excuse me,' I murmured.

So now I'm hearing voices. I could have sworn someone had spoken to me. My optimism had been of very short duration. The present was not a dream, it was reality as harsh as the white walls of the ward that had seemed more welcoming that day. I was getting acclimatised. A man in a grey overall arrived, pushing a smaller trolley than Doudou's. On it were a large aluminium jug, a pile of plastic bowls and a little basket of bread and butter. He put the bowls on the table and poured out a liquid of an indefinable colour.

Monique helped serve, as usual. I couldn't swallow more than a mouthful of this liquid. The other girls seemed to find it quite pleasant to drink.

They ate in silence, without apparent displeasure.

'I say, Sarah, d'you like this stuff?' I asked my neighbour, pointing to my bowl.

'It's coffee. Don't you like it?'

'Oh! With a bit of sugar I might have managed to swallow it, but it's completely tasteless.'

'As far as I'm concerned, the only thing that matters is that it's nice and hot . . .,' she concluded.

The doctors had no round that morning. The chief did his round in our ward once a week, surrounded by his following of assistants and interns – the 'Sorcerer's Apprentices'.

At about ten o'clock Sister Melin came to take me to Dr Edward. She handed me a pair of boots with woolly linings and helped me on with a navy-blue woollen coat. I must have looked a real sight! The coat was too tight and showed about four inches of my nightdress at the bottom; however my feet felt very cosy in the nice warm boots. I was to walk this time, as the wheelchair of the day before had been a favour allowed on the first day of admission, or for very weak patients. The walk and the fresh air invigorated me. The snow that had fallen the previous evening had melted into black slush and I could imagine that my feet were shod in two barges sailing up the Marne, which was represented by the shiny wet asphalt that led from the Pierre Cousin Wing to the building where Dr Edward's office was situated. I felt strangely at peace, a feeling which surprised me as I was not of a nature to give in to things without a fight. Had I any choice? The only thing I could do now was to cooperate with Dr Edward; this at least might get me out of this hospital, and especially this special 'socio-psychological' ward, whose name, according to Sarah, was the futuristic dream of the chief: it was an elegant way of avoiding calling a mongoose a mongoose.

In fact our doctors were all psychiatrists. We were all little embryo lunatics or people for whom madness was the only solution to a desperate situation. Our ward was an observation centre – a shunting yard for adolescents with whose behaviour adults couldn't come to terms. These adults parked us here, probably in order to forget that they were the ones who were responsible for our behaviour and were encouraging it. After a minimum of three months' observation and treatment which might be more or less appropriate one could, according to the severity of one's condition or the progress of the illness, go back to live with one's family, attend a special school or be sent to a psychiatric hospital or, at the worst, for the pathologically hopeless cases, a mental asylum. What direction would I take when I left this shunting yard?

I had to make an effort to keep calm, to control myself. An outburst of rage like the one that had landed me here could lead to the psychiatric hospital, especially in view of my mother's declaration: 'She's completely mad! Put her in a home somewhere, I don't want to see her again!' That's what she'd said to the police.

As on the previous day, we did not have to wait with the outpatients. Sister Melin knocked at the door and we went in without waiting for an answer. Dr Edward was scribbling something on a piece of white paper. He got up this time as soon as we went in and came over to me, all smiles.

'Well! You look splendid today! Not tired any more. . . ?'

'No, doctor, I'm quite all right!'

'That's fine! Today, Sister, I'll call you as soon as we've finished our little chat. We're already old friends. . . .'

When he had shut the door behind her he turned to me.

'Come and lie down, young lady.'

He sat down on the stool beside me.

'Now try and relax thoroughly; here you're with a friend; a doctor isn't a judge. Besides, now that you've got over your anger, I'm sure you see things differently, don't you?'

'Yes. . . .'

'So, you're going to tell me the reason for that terrible outburst. . . .'

'I suppose so. . . .'

I did not know where to begin; I thought he was going to ask me questions and that I'd only have to answer them briefly. . . .

'I expect your troubles only began a month ago, since you got here. So let's begin there,' Dr Edward said to encourage me.

'Yes, doctor. . . .'

'What were your impressions on discovering Paris . . .? Were the people different from those at home?'

'Well, I was glad to be here because I'd come with the intention of continuing my education, which I couldn't do at home. Cocotier hadn't much future for a fisherman's daughter. There were only two alternatives when you left primary school: either to stay at home and see to the housework till you got married, or else get a job as a maid-of-all-work in town and earn between ten and thirty francs' wages, with board, lodging, uniform and free medical attention, according to the people you were lucky enough to work for. In any case, girls who went to work in town came back to the village sooner or later to give birth to a kid they'd got by the master of the house or one of his relatives or friends. I wasn't particularly keen on housework. Neither of these alternatives suited me. Anyway, I don't like Paris. It's too big a city for me. It's a world that's quite unfamiliar to me, with these grey, dirty walls, this murky sky and so many people always in a hurry, always jostling you.'

'Have you had an opportunity of seeing the countryside?' asked Dr Edward.

'Not really. . . .'

'How did you get to Paris?'

'By train. Our boat docked at Le Havre early one morning. We caught a special train that left straight from the harbour, so I didn't see anything of the town. In the train I had a seat in the class that corresponded to the one I'd been in on the boat, in between two fat women. I wasn't near the window, in any case it was misty and I could only catch a glimpse of the countryside. Roger and Mother travelled first class. I met them on the platform when the train got to Saint Lazare station in Paris. . . .'

'Go on, try to remember everything that has happened

since then. Take your time, we're in no hurry,' said Dr Edward.

Roger's flat was five minutes from the station, in General Ofy Street, on the fifth floor of a fairly attractive building, in spite of being the same uniform grey as all the houses. I was struck by the thick, polished wooden entrance door, with its two brass knobs that shone like a mirror in the sun. Roger pressed a little button. In a few seconds the door opened all by itself. A very old lady pulled aside a curtain over a glass door to the right of the entrance hall. When she saw who was there she came to meet us, obviously very pleased to see us. Her smile increased the number of tiny wrinkles round her cheeks that were like two dried prunes. Her eyes blinked cheerfully behind her metal-framed glasses. Her apricot-coloured hair was held back in a black silk net.

'Well now, Mr Milan, so here you are! And Mrs Rosamond! Have you had a good journey?'

'Yes, Mrs Simone.'

'And how's it in the colonies?'

Hm! I thought, 'the colonies'? All these French people in France, don't they know we're a part of France, a French Department . . . or at least an Overseas Province? What's the difference between an Overseas Province and a colony? Come now! What would my friend Charles think? A colony means that you're colonised; that's the same as being dominated, controlled. That makes you think of whips and kicks up the arse, forced labour, and that's only where the present times are concerned. If we talked about the past, it would take us too far back and we'd have to remember our ancestors, the period of slavery and everything that that entails.

No, I prefer to be 'departmentalised', won over, it sounds nicer. It reminds me of Saint-Exupéry's *Little Prince*, with the fox who wanted to be tamed. . . .

'Everything's fine, Mrs Simone,' Roger was replying to the never ending variety of questions that rained down on him.

'And is that where you've brought this little young 'un back from?' she asked, staring at me curiously.

'Oh, yes, this is Zetou, a little cousin,' Mother said, pushing me towards Mrs Simone.

I was stupefied. It couldn't have been worse if the whole building had collapsed around me.

When we got up to the flat Mother busied herself with the luggage and then showed me to my room.

'You understand, Zetou,' she said, 'nobody here knows that I've been married before and that I've got children; so don't be surprised. Roger and I have decided to introduce you as my little cousin that we've adopted, which really means that you'll be our daughter after all.'

'Oh, I understand.'

I was amazed and annoyed, but not hurt. She had been so little of a mother to me that I didn't really feel frustrated.

'What must I call you?' I asked.

'Rosamond . . . at least, Cousin Rosamond, that would be better.'

I didn't dare ask her if I should say Cousin Roger; the idea amused me. A little later on, in the lounge, when I was lost in admiration in front of an impressive radio set, Roger came up to me.

'Would you like to hear it work?'

'Oh yes, please, Cousin Roger. Will you switch it on?'

'Hold on! What's all this about, now! You just call me Roger. "Cousin Roger"! That really sounds like nigger talk.'

I rejoiced inwardly. My poor mother didn't know which way to look. She scowled at me. I couldn't call her Mother or Cousin. After Roger's remark I decided I wouldn't call her anything as I couldn't bring myself to say Rosamond. Still, I wanted to score another point so I said, 'Anyway, why shouldn't I call you "Friend"?'

At home, children call grown-ups 'Friend So-and-so', or just 'Friend'. Mother was squirming. She didn't know whether 'Friend' was nigger talk or not. Roger saved the situation by half approving.

'"Friend" is all right, if you like. But why do you want

to complicate life, Zetou? Call me Roger and your mother Rosamond, that's all. Hello!' (as he looked at his watch) 'It's one o'clock already. We'll go to a restaurant for lunch and then we have some shopping to do. This evening will you do the cooking, Zetou?'

'I don't mind. . . . But I don't know how to make the things you like.'

'Don't worry about that. As far as cooking is concerned, I'm a Creole and I like all our island dishes. Everything really hot and spicy . . . you understand?'

After ten days had elapsed I realised that the 'little cousin' was in fact Roger's and Rosamond's little maid. I did everything, except the washing that they gave out to a laundry. My mother did not re-engage the cleaning woman who used to come once a week before their return to our island. One day when I asked her for the umpteenth time what was happening about entering me for school, she replied, 'I'm really sorry, Zetou, but we got back in the middle of the school year and there are no vacancies. I'll enter you for a correspondence course; I'll help you with the exercises and you can sit for the School Certificate for mature-age students, as you'll soon be sixteen.'

From that day I began to lose heart. As long as I had hopes of going to school I didn't mind doing all the unpleasant jobs. But to know that I was to continue with the housework indefinitely made me lose much of my assurance.

Roger and Rosamond often went out, but they also invited round other Creoles who were fond of punch and Caribbean cooking. Roger was a much better cook than either Mother or me. When we had guests to dinner he came to help me and showed me how to prepare and present a dish nicely, while Mother sat in the lounge smoking her Players and talking in a high-pitched voice in what she hoped was a Parisian accent, to give herself airs of a fine lady.

The guests were nearly always the same people: a Mulatto couple getting on in age, the husband a retired colonial officer who had served in various parts of Africa.

I could never follow the incredible stories that he told, as there were always certain innuendoes that were not clear. However, the tone and the epithets he used showed nothing but contempt for 'niggers who were lazy, dishonest, liars, poisoners,' etc. . . . To listen to him, you'd be hard put to believe that any black blood ran in his veins.

Anemone, his wife, was very beautiful and didn't look a day older than thirty, whereas she was in fact fifty. But, my God! was she stupid! She giggled inanely and asked indiscreet questions. To put everyone at their ease her husband used to say, 'Don't take any notice; I bought this pretty piece of furniture to exhibit in the drawing-room. It's only meant for show,' he would add. My mother was delighted at her friend's silliness as it allowed her to shine.

The other men were all Creoles. Their womenfolk were either half-castes or Europeans except for one pot-bellied widower who came by himself and never took his eyes off me, to my great embarrassment. One day, making the excuse that he was helping me to clear the table, he followed me into the kitchen.

'You are the ray of sunshine that lights up the twilight of my life,' he declared, pressing his enormous paunch against me.

Roger arrived just in time to save me from further embarrassment.

Roger worked with his brother who had a business importing tropical produce. To tell the truth, Roger's brother paid him a salary out of the goodness of his heart and family solidarity, as he only put in two or three hours' appearance a day. He got up when everyone else had almost finished half a day's work. He was usually back home by half past five and sat down immediately to a glass of punch that he prepared himself with great care, following an invariable procedure: first the rum, then a few drops of lemon juice to enhance the flavour and finally two measures of fruit syrup. He had brought back from the Caribbean a collection of fruit syrups specially to make punch with. . . .

A week after the old Creole's grotesque declaration, it

was the day before the last date for returning my exercises to the institution which ran the correspondence course for which Mother had finally enrolled me.

I was struggling to solve a problem when Roger came home from the office about half past four; for once he did not start on his punch.

I could hear him fussing around in the bedroom. Mother had gone out to tea with one of her friends; Roger was to pick her up and then both of them were going to dinner with other friends.

'Zetou, my little treasure, come here a minute!'

I was also the chambermaid and Roger had called me to help him fix his cuff-links.

'Listen, Zetou, my pet . . . I don't think you are going to like this. Our old friend Joseph de la Pierre is mad about you, and it's serious, he wants to marry you. His first wife, my cousin, was a white woman, a complete fool. His only son and heir is sickly; he'd rather have some half-caste offspring that are really strong. He also said something about . . . your being . . . "the last ray of sunshine in the twilight of his life". What do you think?'

I was too flabbergasted to speak, although for once I had the reply on the tip of my tongue, namely that if he had already reached the twilight of his life I was at the dawn of mine, so we had little chance of meeting. In the face of my silence Roger did not know what attitude to take. He walked to and fro, sat down, cleared his throat again and again, as if he were about to make a long speech. I simply stood rooted to the floor in the doorway of his room, like a royal palm tree on a still day.

'You know, I must tell you that it wouldn't be a bad thing for us financially. Joseph will make me a partner when he sets up a new factory to produce guava paste.'

'Oh, good! I'm beginning to understand; you're ready to swap me for a share of guava paste,' I said, breaking my silence.

'Oh, come now, my dear, that's not the case, you don't understand. . . .'

'I've understood perfectly and the answer's no! Definitely no! And especially not with an old white man!'

Roger flushed deep red. I ought to have said simply 'an old man' without adding 'white' and after all that was what I was thinking.

He didn't worry what sort of epithets he would couple with the word 'Negro'.

'Your mother's already given her consent.'

'What!'

'You don't find a son-in-law every day whose pockets are so well lined and who's so open-handed. . . .'

'I'm not surprised at anything any more as far as my mother's concerned, but I thought I'd got a friend in you, especially after I'd confided in you about Charles.'

'Yes . . . Charles, that's another matter . . . I'd rather Rosamond didn't know I've spoken to you about this business.'

After a brief glance at his watch, Roger put on his jacket and pushed quickly past me and left the house. Why was he suddenly in such a hurry?

If I was badly shaken by the news of this marriage that Roger and Mother had cooked up, I still did not think that all was lost. I couldn't quite see how Mother could marry me off against my will. My real worry was why I hadn't heard from Charles.

Since my arrival in France I had written him five letters in less than four weeks and I had only received one from our village and that was from Zelia who, strangely enough, made no mention of Charles or of his family. I had given my letters to Roger to post. 'Charles, that's another matter,' he had said. What was the meaning of this other matter? What was I to understand by this?

During the next two days I never had a chance to speak to Roger alone and my mother made no mention of Joseph de la Pierre or of Charles. Then Roger, making the excuse that he was tired, refused to accompany Mother to a concert. I would have loved to go . . . but Mother didn't suggest taking me and I didn't dare ask her. She was ashamed of me; she was always afraid I wouldn't know how to behave or that I'd ask embarrassing questions that she couldn't answer.

I was much more at ease with Roger. He loved our island, our customs, our food; we often had discussions without any embarrassment. I thought he was really quite a nice person, although he did use rather unpleasant words to describe Negroes when he talked about them. But I sensed that it was his usual way of speaking rather than any indication that he really looked down on them.

So I stayed behind with Roger, quite determined to have it out with him during the three hours that Mother would be away.

'Roger, you've got to tell me. . . .'

'What now? I've told you all I know; now you must wait for your mother to speak to you.'

'I mean about Charles. I've had no news. Did you post my letters?'

'Very well, listen. As far as your Charles is concerned, you can say goodbye to him. By the time a kid of sixteen is old enough to get married, he'll have changed his mind and you'll stay an old maid.'

'That's my problem; that doesn't explain why I haven't received any letters.'

Roger got up from his chair and came slowly towards me, staring hard as if he'd never seen me before. He grasped my two hands and pulled me to my feet. 'Have you looked at yourself in the mirror?' he said. 'You can turn many a head in Paris.' And pulling me to him he kissed me on the forehead.

'Tell me! Do you know why I don't get any letters, please?' I asked, adopting a more beseeching tone.

By way of an answer he hugged me tightly to him. Up till then I had not been aware of what was happening. Now I was afraid, without knowing why. I tried to free myself. He held me even tighter and said breathlessly, in a hoarse voice that I didn't recognise, 'Don't move, my little treasure, it does me good to have you here; I haven't known such happiness for a long time.'

I soon grew tired in my struggle to free myself. I felt a great shame; my heart beat so violently that it hurt. I felt myself sinking into a black bottomless pit and a moment later I was aware that I was lying on the carpet with Roger on top of me.

I opened my eyes. He kissed me on the lips. I could not move. I had neither the strength nor the will. Something hurt, a burning inside me.

'You're not angry with me, my little treasure?' I couldn't understand what he meant or what had happened to me.

He got up slowly and it was then that I realised that something very strange had occurred. I had just been reborn in a topsy-turvy world in which the mongoose turns into a wolf to devour the kid; and the latter's only weapons are bitter tears.

'Come now, my pet, say something!'

I had nothing to say. It no longer mattered that I didn't receive any letters from Charles. Besides I wouldn't write to him any more. I was no longer worthy of him. . . .

As if by chance, Mother went out every afternoon for a week and Roger came home every day earlier and earlier, more and more affectionate, more and more pressing.

I couldn't manage to hate him; I even felt a certain affection for him, in spite of myself, for this man was my only friend in this Parisian jungle. He seemed worried about our situation. Whereas he used to be full of fun and was always laughing and joking, he was now very serious and sometimes quite touching.

'You are the most precious, the purest thing in my life. Nothing will ever be the same for me again . . .,' he said one day.

As far as I was concerned, I tried not to think about what had happened to me, it couldn't be a real fact. We were two actors in a play, acting a comedy which had nothing to do with our lives. When we left the stage we would resume our real roles and I would start thinking about Charles again and the future we had mapped out for ourselves as long as I could remember. . . .

'Zetou, the first time I spoke to you about Joseph de la Pierre I could only see your mother's interests and mine. Now, it's the only solution I can find to our joint happiness. We can continue to see each other without anyone suspecting anything.'

'I can't. Don't speak to me about it again.'

'Materially, your situation will be very enviable. . . .'

'How can you imagine me living with that man? He disgusts me. . . . And his money too.'

'Actually he's quite nice, and you'll have me near you every day.'

'Please Roger, don't let's talk about it any more. I'm not capable of thinking or making any decision. I don't want anything. . . . Or rather, if we could build a world to our liking, I'd rather be back home, dreaming of my future life with Charles and never having known any of you, including you and your friend Joseph.'

'One thing's certain, and that is that Joseph is really in love with you. And that's more than I can say about your friend Charles.'

'Charles has got nothing to do with this problem. It's because of you that I've had to give him up.'

'You're wrong, my dear. . . .'

Roger had a nasty gleam in his eyes. He went to his bedroom and came back with an envelope in his hands.

'Very well then, I'll tell you everything about your Charles: the first letter that your mother received went into the dustbin. I don't know what it contained but your mother wrote back to Charles something along the lines of "Dear Sir, I didn't bring my daughter to Europe so that she could continue to associate with a little nigger-boy like you, etc." Before you blame your mother, I'll show you a letter we received a few days ago from your sister. Your mother didn't give it to you; it's about her letter to Charles. She was wrong for once, as this letter shows that she had acted correctly. Read it yourself.'

He held out a letter to me. I foresaw that its contents would add to my distress. But I had to know and continue the adventure to the end. . . .

'Dear Zetou, you still haven't answered my previous letter. I suppose you've got so much to see and do that you've quite forgotten us. Unless you didn't get my letter.

'In my previous letter I told you that Father has finally let me go back to school for two years, until I get my primary certificate. I'm very pleased, as that's all I wanted, not being ambitious like you. My future doesn't go any further than our village and the surroundings, I'm afraid of big towns.

'You don't have to worry about Charles. If he hadn't received that famous letter from Mother, he'd naturally have gone on writing to you, but in any case you didn't come into his plans for the future any more.

'For the past year he has been in love with a colonel's daughter who's in the same class as him at school. This girl has travelled a lot, to every continent. She was born in Indochina. We saw her in Cocotier last Sunday. She was with her father who had come to give a medal to Papa Mano for his son Gerard who was killed in the last war. After the ceremony there was a reception in the village hall.

'Charles was invited with his father and he put on important airs as all the other village children could only look through the windows in silence. The girl isn't a bit pretty, she's got legs as straight as coconut palm trunks and thick glasses and what's more her hair is cut short like a boy's.

'Charles looked very proud of himself as she's a colonel's daughter.

'Apart from this, life in the village is still the same of course; in less than a month there's been no particular changes.

'Father, Grandma, Jose, Louis and I all send our love and I send lots of kisses.

'P.S. Mrs Felix sends her regards; she says whatever the future holds in store for you, you'll always be her little girl. She's very fond of you. Send her a little note as soon as you can.'

This was one more link in my chain of misfortunes. I would have preferred to go on believing that only Roger and Mother were responsible for Charles's silence, since I had already put aside my young love for him, feeling that I was no longer worthy of it. I could scarcely believe what Zelia wrote; this girl was only a schoolfriend.

There was no proof that Charles was in love with her. The village folk had just jumped to conclusions about her arrival in their midst.

How could Charles forget me so quickly for a stranger? We were moulded from the same sulphurous clay from the foot of the volcano. We had taken our first stumbling steps together, laughed at the same things, liked the same games, the same stories. . . .

'Well, Zetou, what do you think of that?'

'Anyway, I'm not worthy of him any more.'

'Come now, don't dramatise things. . . .You've got your life before you and me at your feet. . . . Not to mention Joseph who adores you,' Roger said teasingly.

He could afford to take things lightly as nothing was dramatic for him. But I knew that things had to come to a head and that the end could only be to my disadvantage.

This letter had shaken me more than I could say. I was no longer on a stage, playing my part opposite other actors. The curtain would never fall, never, as I was playing my own role.

How I would love to find refuge once more in the bottom of Father's boat. . . !

From that day I turned in on myself more than ever and refused to go out of the house. In the streets I felt lost. I was overwhelmed by a profound, infinite depression at the sight of girls of my own age walking past, arm in arm, laughing and carefree. The only worries they could have would be over their schoolwork. They were in their own country, surrounded by family and friends.

Whereas I was a solitary piece of flotsam, washed along by life, with nothing to catch on to.

In this city the only family and friends I had were a mother-cousin and a stepfather-lover. Years seemed to have passed since I had left my hut, so rich and warm with affection, my village, my sun. There I had wept. All the world over children weep. I had had my childhood sorrows. But I had never known this total solitude of the soul which envelops the whole being in an armour of despair. I was only sixteen and the future was filled with bad omens. . . .

As the sorcerer had said: 'The gods of Africa were not favourable.' Why had I left my country. . . ?

Roger was my only friend. As the days went by, surrounded by his affection, I attached myself more and more closely to him. Was I in love with him? Certainly not. I couldn't quite make out the nature of my feelings for him. The idea of marrying Joseph de la Pierre and keeping on my liaison with Roger made me shudder with horror.

What had happened to the moral principles and the ideas of right and wrong that Father John had driven into us with clouts and cuffs at the Thursday catechism classes? I hadn't been to Mass since my arrival in Paris. Neither Mother nor Roger were practising Catholics. Imperceptibly I had grown away from the Church, from God and the idea of sin. I had never believed that I was sinning. I was sharing a man with my mother, I was damning my own soul, and this thought upset me. For the first time I felt that I was really guilty of something monstrous.

I got out of bed, knelt down and in a short but fervent prayer begged God to forgive me. I decided to marry Joseph and be faithful to him, to take pity on his age in order to expiate my fault by overcoming every day the physical revulsion I felt for him. Tears of repentance flowed from my eyes and I remained kneeling a long time at the foot of my bed, feeling guilty, terribly guilty.

The idea of what I must now tell Dr Edward made me burst into tears. 'Doctor, all that is nothing to what I discovered three days ago.' Tears choked me and I could not go on with my story. Dr Edward took my hand.

'Come now! A little more courage, Zetou. You can rely on me. I will help you, not like I help all my patients that

I see here, but like a brother. You must tell me everything, it will make you feel much better. . . .'

'Thank you, doctor.'

I remained silent for a moment, trying to create a void within myself, so as to stop my sobs. Finally I took up the thread of my story.

So, Doctor, I might have forgiven Mother for holding back Charles's letters, thinking it was for my own good, to avoid my being even more disillusioned later; I might have forgiven her for wanting me to marry a man who was old enough to be her own father, to assure me of a future without any material wants; I might have managed to forgive her all that, but . . . three days ago, when I was still kneeling at the foot of my bed, accusing myself of having a heart black with sin, I heard Roger and Mother come in. It must have been three or four o'clock in the morning. The hall door was open, as well as my bedroom door. I didn't like being shut in. I was accustomed to sleeping with my sister in a room that had no door.

I could hear everything they were saying. They must have drunk a lot, to judge by Mother's nervous giggle. Curiosity was greater than my desire to get back into my warm bed. I got to my feet and peered down the hall to see what they were doing. They were sitting on the divan in the lounge and Roger had his arm round Mother's waist. He had poured his usual glass of punch, in spite of the fact that it was early morning.

'Look, Roger, as soon as we've got old Joseph to take my nuisance of a daughter off our hands, let's get him to pay for a little holiday in Rio for the Carnival.'

'I won't say no,' replied Roger.

'Anyway, you've got to make some amends for all the fun you've had with the little sucker. I suppose she's busy dreaming of you right now, her Prince Charming!'

'Shut up!' Roger said, pretending to be annoyed. 'You're getting fiendishly maternal!'

They looked at each other and burst out laughing.

It was their laughter more than anything else that sent

me into a furious rage. Suddenly I realised how I had been duped. I had been seduced by Roger with my mother's connivance and sold like a slave to an old white man. A feeling of hatred that I had never felt before blurred my vision – hatred for these two people against whom I now hurled myself, but also hatred for all the white people who had always deceived us, humiliated and mocked us, since my first ancestor was wrenched from his African coast.

When she saw me Mother let out a scream, so attracting my attention more particularly to her. I was propelled by a force over which my reason had no control. Our struggle made sufficient noise to alert the neighbours who immediately called the police.

Roger made no move to separate us. He calmly drained his glass and went to open the door when the police arrived. Mother managed to free herself.

'Take her away, she's completely mad, she wants to kill me, I'm her mother!'

She was weeping and moaning. I was completely nauseated and couldn't stop myself spitting on the carpet, which made her cry out in horror.

'Oh! You see, she's crazy!'

Two policemen flung themselves upon me. I struggled furiously and screamed back all my helplessness. One of the policemen slapped me. Far from calming down, I bit him. The two policemen had to carry me down the five flights of stairs.

The police station was not far from General Ofy Street, only a few hundred yards from the house. They shoved me into a sort of barred cage, separated into two parts; the section I was in had a long wooden bench on which two women were sitting, probably prostitutes by the look of their painted faces and their far from discreet get-up. The other half was occupied by a grey-faced man who looked sad and resigned. He wore an old overcoat that must once have been a metallic blue and his shoes were covered in mud. One of my neighbours called to the policeman on duty who was sitting at a little table in front of us, reading a magazine.

'I say, ducky, give us a cigarette,' she asked.

'Smoking's not allowed here.'

'There's such a stink here that I'm going to throw up,' she said.

'It's that filthy wog who stinks,' the policeman replied. 'I can't help you – the inspector won't allow any smoking.'

I was dressed only in my flannelette pyjamas and had no slippers on. As soon as my fury had abated I began to feel terribly cold and I was shivering violently. The blonde noticed and called the policeman again.

'I say, old cock, haven't you got a pullover or something for the kid? Her teeth are chattering.'

'No!'

'She'll catch her death!'

'I don't give a shit. They can all go to hell, wogs and niggers and chinks!'

The blonde got up and made me sit between the two of them to try to get warm; the other woman took off a scarf she was wearing round her neck and put it over my shoulders. I felt much better. About eight o'clock the two women and the man in the next compartment were let out. I was left all alone, exhausted, incapable of thinking, very aware of the reality around me. I had chosen a broad flowery road and it had changed into a narrow path filled with ambushes. But I had to keep on along this path. I had no other possible choice. . . .

At about midday a policeman brought me a sandwich, a dress and a pair of shoes that my mother must have sent.

I put the dress on over my pyjamas and rolled the legs up as far as my knees. I had no coat. The policeman took me out to the yard of the police station and made me get into a small car. He sat next to me on the back seat; another policeman arrived and got in at the other door. In this way I was well wedged in; the driver set off. After a good half hour's ride we drove into the courtyard of an imposing building. The policeman who had brought my dress led me into a waiting room. He handed some documents over to another policeman who was on guard at the entrance and then went off.

There were some other youngsters there, four boys and two girls. Two of the boys sat next to men dressed in long black gowns. They were talking in an undertone. The girls were each accompanied by someone who seemed to be a parent, a father or a mother. The policeman on duty in the room pointed to an empty chair next to a little grey-haired old woman who was with a girl of fifteen or sixteen. Except for the two boys and the men in black, nobody said a word. Their faces were serious and worried. I was probably the calmest, not having any idea what was in store for me.

On the door in front of me was a notice saying 'Judge Perle'. A man wearing a different uniform from the policemen called a name. The old woman next to me got up and went into the judge's office, followed by the girl.

I was the last to be called before the judge. The clock in the waiting room said half past five. I was tired, very tired, aching all over and starving. I had refused the sandwich at the police station at midday. The man in uniform showed me into a small room. The judge was seated, impressive in his severity, behind an enormous desk. He had grey hair and was wearing a dazzling white shirt under a black satin waistcoat with a black tie. Another man was sitting at an ancient typewriter placed on a little table near the door. The judge examined me as I walked towards him. At the sight of his hostile and contemptuous expression I realised I could expect no comfort from that direction.

'Surname? First name? Age?'

The typewriter started up at the same time as this cascade of questions. As each key was struck, it echoed in my head and empty stomach, confusing me. The judge read a long report from the police station, with my mother's statement. She pointed out, among other things, that she was very worried by my behaviour and the things I had said since my arrival in France and simply asked the judge to put me in some institution where I could be looked after. Roger, like all weak personalities, had not found it necessary to give his personal opinion. He had simply approved everything that my mother had said.

I jumped up, outraged to hear this slander.

'But that's completely untrue!' I shouted.

'Sit down. you ought to be ashamed of yourself, young woman. You struck your mother without cause. You are quite mad.'

I was so sickened by all these lies that I was incapable of speaking calmly in my own defence. So I began to shout the judge down.

'Be quiet! Guard, take this wildcat away.'

I was desperate and screamed with rage and impotence in the face of this one-sided judgement. The guard dragged me down a long dark corridor to the sick bay where they gave me an injection and I knew nothing more until I woke up here the next morning. . . .

When I had finished my story I felt calm and very tired, exhausted and emptied, like the shell of a calabash. I closed my eyes and felt as though I were melting away, like the half-pound of lard I had left one day on a rock out in the sun. It had melted right away and sunk into the ground and disappeared. The only trace left behind was a piece of greasy paper.

I needed to have a bath. It would be my purgatory: I would be washed clean of all my impurity. I began to daydream:

> I have no desires
> Except to sleep for ever
> I have no desires
> Except to sail away
> In a little boat and not return
> I have no desires
> Except from my boat to cast adrift
> All my chains and all my loves.

I opened my eyes. Dr Edward was talking. I was not listening to him and yet, in spite of myself, I heard words which made no sense as other words were missing. Those that my mind had not caught in its exhaustion. Reliving my drama had not brought me the relief that Dr Edward had supposed. I was more desperate than ever. I had lost my will to fight, lost all notion of time and place. I was as limp as a jack-in-the-box that has lost its springs, meeker than a toothless cat without claws.

When I got back to our ward I found my suitcase on my bed and a letter from Zelia.

> 'Dear Zetou, A great calamity struck us last Saturday. It rained all day and all the roads were flooded. For some reason or other Mr Felix's bus skidded off the road on to the verge and fell over a cliff. Mr Felix and Charles were badly hurt and were dead when help arrived. Jose lost an arm and had a lot of other injuries, his life is not in danger; he's being looked after in hospital in town.'

Then followed a list of the other passengers who were dead or injured. . . .

A few days or a few hours earlier, this news would have shattered me. Now. . . no feeling could penetrate my armour of despair. . . .

I was plunged into an alien world, behind a wall of darkness. I could hear people talking and laughing on the other side, but I could not communicate with them. My tongue felt thick and painful. I opened my mouth but no sound came. I was slipping slowly into a bottomless abyss. My first impression was that I was happy to be far from the others, sheltered by my wall.

But when I realised that at the bottom of the abyss was death, I struggled desperately to get out. The room I entered was empty. A quantity of empty glasses, plates and bottles piled miserably everywhere, indicated that an important celebration had been taking place there.

Something caught my attention. It was a little sprig of orange blossom, still smelling sweetly. It lay on the ground like a pearl on a rubbish heap.

It was too late. There was nobody there. I was still alone. Once more I could feel myself slipping down into a chasm. This time I made no attempt to halt my descent into the valley of darkness. When I reached the bottom I was aware of lying in the bottom of a boat.

The only thing I could see from the bottom of the boat was a man's broad naked back – his glistening muscles, wet with perspiration, were reassuring in their strength – and a tiny white cloud hanging in a blue sky.

Danny Boy

James Bradner

Danny and Lily are childhood sweethearts, growing up together in Guyana. No matter that Danny is black, while Lily is Indian and their friendship frowned upon by her father. They know they are right for each other, and their love is tender and true.

But envious eyes are watching and waiting in the shadows . . . and this is one love story that does not have a happy ending.

Drumbeat 36
ISBN 0 582 78536 7